Saved by Scandal

Saved by Scandal

ANGELA JOHNSON

SWEETWATER BOOKS
An imprint of Cedar Fort, Inc.
Springville, Utah

This is a work of fiction. The characters, names, incidents, places, and dialogue are products of the author's imagination and are not to be construed as real. The opinions and views expressed herein belong solely to the author and do not necessarily represent the opinions or views of Cedar Fort, Inc. Permission for the use of sources, graphics, and photos is also solely the responsibility of the author.

ISBN 13: 978-1-4621-3943-9

Published by Sweetwater Books, an imprint of Cedar Fort, Inc.
2373 W. 700 S., Springville, UT 84663
Distributed by Cedar Fort, Inc., www.cedarfort.com

Library of Congress Control Number: 2021931757

Cover design by Shawnda T. Craig
Cover design © 2021 Cedar Fort, Inc.
Edited by Valene Wood and Rachel Hathcock
Typeset by Valene Wood

Printed in the United States of America

10 9 8 7 6 5 4 3 2 1

Printed on acid-free paper

For my Mom.
For reading my books, even though they are fiction.
For loving me, even when I am difficult.
I'm thankful you are my mom.
I love you.

Chapter 1

The Duke of Ashby, her father, had to be insane. Charlotte shook with confused exasperation. "I vow I will not dance with him if he were the last man in Derbyshire!"

Marianne laughed, holding her stomach as if she'd never heard anything so amusing. "Poor Lord Riley. He will find a house of disagreeable women upon his arrival."

"I cannot believe father added him to the list." Phillip looked to their mother in abject horror. "What was he thinking?"

"You know Ashby and his need for a specific society." The excuses were old and always the same.

Charlotte understood it was the woman's place to support her husband but how far did a woman have to go for such a disagreeable man? Her mother stood beside Ashby and agreed with every decision he made, even when they were questionable. Charlotte loved her mother and even her father, but that did not mean she would marry a disagreeable man just because her father put him in front of her.

Phillip paced the room. "Riley is a rake, Mother. How dare he invite such a man to his home where his daughters reside. I would take my wife and sisters to Arundel Keep for the summer if I had not invited my own acquaintances."

"Calm down, Phillip." It was strange to hear Edward speaking with calmness. Charlotte wanted him to stand against their father to save her from an imprudent match. "We will keep a watchful eye on Riley and prevent him from pursuing our sisters."

Charlotte let out a very unladylike harrumph. "I dare say there will not be a need as neither one of us will encourage him."

"I do hope you plan to encourage at least one young man during this house party," her mother said, looking as though it were a command and not a general thought.

"I suppose it depends on who has been invited. If all the men in the party are rakes and rouges, I would prefer to be a burden on my family as a spinster." Charlotte knew she should not have said the words, but her mother's comments encouraged her flippancy.

"You are entering your fifth season. You must find a husband this year." The stress in her mother was evident. It would not do for her to have a spinster daughter. "Arundel, convince your sister of her need for a match."

"Mother, I am only two and twenty. I am not yet on the shelf." The insinuation was not only hurtful but had a ring of truth to it. With her fifth season approaching, the admirers would be focused on her dowry more than her person and she did not care for a man who wanted fortune more than love.

Phillip patted their mother's hand. "Do not fear, Mother. If there comes a time for Charlotte to relocate, she may stay at Arundel Keep with Emma and me."

"You mean to tease me, Arundel, but I assure you I am not of the humor. Your sisters both need to find husbands, and with haste."

"Is there a reason it must be done this season?" Phillip looked concerned.

"Your father will not wait through another season before he matches Charlotte, and I fear it will be with Lord Riley."

The information was distressing to Charlotte, yet the effect it had on all three of her brothers was more of disgust and anger. Phillip, Edward, and Charles burst out at the same moment, each with their own comments. The general consensus was that they would work to find her a husband. Charlotte did not like being the topic of conversation but had no way to stop the course of action. She would refuse Lord Riley if their father tried to match them. She would run away, never to return to Wentworth Hall if need be.

"I also fear your father will have need of speaking with you, Arundel." Their mother spoke with great care so as not to anger her eldest son.

"What have I done now?" Phillip said with a small laugh. Charlotte knew it was to stave off the nervousness of having their father focused on him. Since he had left Wentworth Hall to reside in Sussex with his wife, Ashby had little to comment or remark upon.

"I had hope," Ashby said entering the parlor, "you and your wife would share your great fortune with us." A visible tension fell over the occupants as no one ever knew Ashby's true intent.

"What *fortune* would you be referring to, your grace?" Phillip bowed respectfully in their father's direction.

"You do your family an injustice by delaying in filling a nursery." Ashby didn't have a shameful bone in his body. He spoke as though it were a conversation to be had in front of the entire family.

Charlotte tried to look away from Emma, Lady Arundel, as her sister-in-law blushed deeply. Emma knew when she married the heir to Ashby's title and estate, the duke would be tiresome and intruding, but Charlotte didn't know how they could handle such invasion of privacy. But then she remembered her mother's subtle warning to make a match. Anger stirred in her chest, her breath tight as she realized Ashby was intruding in her life as well. What to do, she didn't know, but allowing Ashby to find her a husband was out of the question. He'd choose poorly.

"Your Grace," Phillip said with a glare of distrust toward their father, "when we have anything to share, we will send you a letter."

"I do hope it is soon. You have a duty to your family." Ashby sat in his chair with the London News, ignoring the rest of the conversation. Charlotte took a moment to view her family. She wondered if the house party her mother planned was a wise venture given Ashby's anger over a lack of an heir. Anyone who knew Ashby would notice the storm brewing in his eyes and his rigid posture of disapproval.

Charlotte admired Lord Haughton as he exited the carriage. He was tall, dark haired, and terribly handsome. For the first time since her mother told the family about the house party and the conversation about her need to marry, she decided it was a good idea.

"Lord Haughton, my sisters Lady Charlotte and Lady Marianne." Both curtsied. Charlotte smiled hoping he'd take notice of her beauty. Taking inventory of her dress, she wished she'd chosen the purple instead of green. Green was fine, but she preferred the way the purple made her feel, and she always received compliments when wearing it. A small excitement erupted in her heart as she recognized the flutter of anticipation. She wanted a compliment from Lord Haughton. *What a terrible decision to go with green!*

Charlotte listened to Phillip as he introduced the rest of their guests. Lord Haughton had two sisters, Lillian and Hazel. Both were beautiful, but they were sisters. She did another mental check to make certain her smile did not show her pleasure at his singleness. This party really was a wonderful idea.

As she met their guests throughout the day, there were not any of the single men who compared to Lord Haughton. Charlotte did not care about his title or his wealth, she noticed his handsomeness, but he also seemed kind and good. Her brothers would not be friends with anyone who wasn't upstanding, so she could trust the man.

By supper time, the house was full of guests, most of them high-ranking members of the peerage, which met her father's need for socializing. Dukes, duchesses, marquess, and earls walked the halls of Wentworth. If not for the hope of turning Lord Haughton's eyes to her, Charlotte would have dressed in a plain gown. But for dinner, she chose the gold evening dress her mother procured for her to impress a gentleman and convince him of a future. Charlotte decided Lord Haughton was the man. She wondered, as she checked her reflection one last time, what her mother would do once she no longer had single daughters to marry off.

Walking into the parlor, she noticed Lord Haughton and smiled in his direction, her heart pounding with hope of speaking to him without making a fool of herself. Crossing the room, Charlotte held herself with grace and poise, focused on her destination. The room seemed small with the added people in the house, yet grand as the pounding in her heart made the distance never ending and the anticipation of the conversation drying out her mouth. As she walked, her foot hit something hard, knocking her off balance. Charlotte tried to catch herself but found the floor racing toward her face as arms wrapped around her waist. Thankful she didn't hit the ground. Charlotte looked up to see her protector. "Thank you, Collin."

"You are most welcome, my lady."

"How fortunate I am to have you standing here."

"Yes, my lady."

She gave him a thankful nod of the head and walked away. Collin was such a kind man. He'd been a footman at their home for just over a year and Charlotte liked him. She wished they could be friends, but with the difference in their stations, it was not possible.

"Lady Charlotte, what happened? I cannot imagine the terror of falling in front of everyone. Although, you would have garnered much attention if that horrible servant had not manhandled you," Lady Violet said taking hold of her arm.

"Collin is a good man, Lady Violet, and I am thankful he was available to assist me. I would not want to tumble to the ground no matter the amount of attention it would have provided." Attention from misfortune was not the consideration she looked for from men. She wanted Lord Haughton to notice her based on her beauty, intellect, and demeanor.

"I cannot even imagine the distress this must have brought on you." She pulled her brother over, "Riley, please escort Lady Charlotte to the sofa. She has experienced a terrible fall."

"I am well enough and am not in need of any assistance." The last person Charlotte wanted near her was Lord Riley. The man was a brute.

"Lady Charlotte, I insist on helping you to a seat." Riley gave a lascivious smile, sending shivers of displeasure through her body. She would need to be on her guard.

"Thank you, but no." Stern and unmoving, Charlotte would refuse any offer of help as she had no desire to associate with the man. He was here as Ashby's guest, and there would be no mingling on her part, if she could help it.

"I would not wish you to fall again." Riley's smile deepened, showing his teeth while giving an heir of malevolence.

"I have no intention of falling, Lord Riley." The nervousness she'd experienced earlier was replaced with the desire to escape. If she could leave the party and spend the evening with the horses or in her chambers, she'd find more comfort than exploring ways to avoid Lord Riley.

"I find women who avoid me are the most desirable."

"And I find men like you to be despicable." Hiding her dislike wouldn't do any good. If she let him know her feelings to begin with, perhaps she could avoid the discomfort bound to be in her future with the man.

Charlotte turned away to see Lord Haughton again standing in the same spot. Losing her courage, she found solace in the company of her sisters. Emma, Marianne, and Anne stood waiting for her.

Chapter 2

"Arundel, I must admit I did not expect a house party with so many guests." Haughton looked around the room to gauge the level of peerage he was spending time with.

"My mother's idea." Arundel looked thinner than he once had. Of course, the previous two years had been hard on him. He thought the earl had healed, but there was still a haunted look around his eyes. Or perhaps Garrett only imagined it because he knew the situation.

"It is nice not being in London at this time. A late summer party was a fabulous idea."

"Lady Arundel and I were not planning a visit to London this year."

"Does not Ashby expect you in town?"

"I have used my health as an excuse, since Emma and I were married. He has not fought me on the subject."

"I must admit this does surprise me, but I am happy to hear your circumstances have changed for the better."

"You should visit Arundel Keep. We would love to host you for the winter."

"I do not know if it will be possible this year, but another year would be nice."

This comment brought Lord Arundel's attention fully on their conversation. "You have plans already? I must admit I find this surprising."

Trying to take the conversation in a different direction, as Garrett didn't want to admit the reasons he'd be tied up for the holiday, he said the only words to enter his mind. "Your sister Lady Charlotte looks beautiful tonight."

Phillip raised an eyebrow as he looked toward his sister. "She does. Good eye, Garrett." Phillip patted him on the back to show there were no ill feelings for the admiration of his sister. "Perhaps I will introduce your younger sisters to my brother Charles, he's in need of a wife."

Garrett laughed, "I have no doubt Lillian would love an introduction. She did not stop talking about the handsome Lord Charles the entire trip. Cholmondeley nearly had an apoplexy when she declared her admiration."

"Does your father not intend to allow a match for her?" Phillip's question was said in jest, for the most part.

"Cholmondeley expects me to make a match. As the heir to the marquess, I am required to do so. But his daughters have time." His words came without thought—words he'd hoped to keep quiet for the time.

Phillip patted him on the shoulder. "Then make haste, Lord Haughton. We would not want you to be a lonely bachelor much longer."

"I must admit, I am not lonely. My sisters keep me entertained quite well." Garrett found Arundel's wife with his eyes. "Do you enjoy being married?"

"Very much so. I could not have made a better match."

"Now you mention it, will we be seeing the illustrious Duke and Duchess of Norland at this house party?"

"No." Phillip paused for a moment before continuing. Garrett wondered if he should have left the comment for another time. It was a sensitive subject. "They are staying in Sheffield."

"A relief, I am sure."

"Yes, their presence calls my father's anger up on the matter and reminds him of what he could have had, if only I had been a more dutiful son."

"I heard you were not disinherited."

"No, my father never intended to do anything so drastic."

Garrett quirked his eyebrow. "Really? Ashby?"

Phillip laughed, "Of course. It would be far too scandalous, and we were already the talk of society."

Not sure where to take the awkward conversation, Garrett let out a breath he didn't realize he was holding as Lady Arundel and Lady

Charlotte approached. He bowed and acknowledged the pleasantries while admiring Lady Charlotte and the way she shined in the gold dress she wore. Admiring beautiful women was one of the best parts of the season and house parties.

"Lord Haughton, do you plan to spend your time hunting during this party? Or will you make time for other pursuits?" Lady Arundel asked with the most innocent look on her face. Somehow Garrett knew there was an underlying question.

"I am at the mercy of my hosts, my lady. I will do as Ashby expects."

Lady Arundel exchanged a mischievous smile with Lady Charlotte, causing him a bit of unrest. Lady Charlotte looked very handsome, but he was not ready to be caught in a tryst with her. *Such a random thought!* He'd never feared such a situation before this moment. Finding a way to change the conversation, he asked, "Is anyone else set to arrive? Or is this the entire party?"

Phillip responded, "I believe the Duke and Duchess of Dudley will be here on the marrow with their daughter Lady Ruby. But they are the last."

"Ah, yes, it would not be a party without Dudley." Garrett smiled to let them know he was jesting. His next comment on Lady Ruby was cut off as the butler announced it was time to go into dinner.

"Lord Haughton, would you be so kind as to escort Charlotte for us?" Lady Arundel asked with such innocence he was certain she was asking out of courtesy.

"It would be my honor."

"Thank you, Lord Haughton." Charlotte had a small twinge of a blush creeping into her cheeks as she locked eyes with Lady Arundel. Nevertheless, she took his arm and he escorted her into dinner.

Dinner was wonderful, especially with the conversation. He and Lady Charlotte spoke as though they'd been friends their entire lives. When the ladies left for the parlor, Garrett found Phillip and Edward. Although he knew the other men in the party, he was closest with the twins.

"Is there a plan for tomorrow?" he asked, hoping to keep the conversation light.

"There will be a small hunting party in the morning," Edward responded. "What were you and Charlotte speaking on during dinner? There never seemed a silent moment."

I am trapped! he thought. *I never should have mentioned my father's desire for me to marry.* "There was not a specific topic. Pleasantries. Similar to what I would say to my sister."

It wasn't exactly true. They'd discussed the weather, which was a dull topic, but quickly turned it into a discussion on riding. He hoped to ask Charlotte to ride with him during this visit, but that information was not for Arundel or Edward.

"Pleasantries?" Edward said with startling disappointment. His face contorted in displeasure.

Arundel handed him a glass to refresh his drink. "Haughton, if you plan to find a wife, you will need to come up with something more interesting to speak of during dinner. Try speaking of Shakespeare."

Edward shook his head. "Lottie likes Shakespeare, but it is not a way to woo her."

Woo her? Garrett needed to find a way to change the conversation as he did not care to speak of courting their sister. He only met her earlier that day. He was of course attracted to the lady, but he had a penchant to fight the connection, and he didn't know why. "I admit I have little interest in wooing a woman by using Shakespeare."

"A disappointment indeed!" Arundel said with a shake of his head.

Nodding his head in agreement, he listened as the twins disappointedly changed back to the conversation of the hunt and the purpose of the house party. When it was time to enter the parlor with the ladies, Garrett chose a game table and spent his evening in a whist tournament with his younger sister, Hazel, as his partner. They lost, not because of the lack of knowledge on how to play the game, but because Haughton was too busy watching Lord Madden and Lord Potts while they flirted with Charlotte. *It is curious, why am I jealous of the men speaking with her? Perhaps a tryst with the lady would not be a bad idea after all,* he thought as he laid the losing card on the table.

Chapter 3

Charlotte smiled at her reflection. Molly took the appropriate time with the hot iron curling the strands of hair dangling out of the coiffure, making the blond dazzle with her complexion. Perfect enough for Charlotte to impress Lord Haughton. She thought back over their conversation at dinner the night before. He enjoyed painting as much as she did. He loved to ride his horse, as did she. Those were the only two things they found commonality in, but it was enough for now. Smoothing down her dark blue riding habit, she hurried from the room, not wanting to keep Lord Haughton waiting. He was to go painting with her.

She walked into the yard to see Lord Haughton with their horses saddled and painting supplies packed. He'd even found a chaperone, which happened to be the footman Collin. Since the party was waiting for Lord Dudley and his family to arrive, they had one more day of rest before the serious hunting began. Charlotte planned to make the most out of the little time she had with him. Her mother wanted her married, to prevent Ashby from swindling a deal through a game of cards, and Charlotte planned to make it a man she could love.

"Lady Charlotte, may I help you mount?"

"Thank you, my lord."

"Do you have a specific place where you paint?"

Charlotte smiled at him, she wanted him to admire her, but hoped she didn't look or sound wanton. These types of situations had to be done with care to secure a proposal. "I usually go to the meadow. There is a lovely little river and the most beautiful trees."

"Then I must beg you to lead the way."

Charlotte nodded and worked to keep excitement hidden while he was watching her. She didn't want him to think she was a silly girl with nothing in her head except the hope of marriage.

Charlotte listened as Lord Haughton hummed a tune throughout their ride. *Is he as nervous as I?* She snuck a peek at him when certain he wasn't watching and kept a smile on her face, doing a mental check every once in a while to make certain it was genuine instead of forced. Her heart raced with each movement of his head. The expectation of what could happen by being persuasive and encouraging brought hope and fear to her heart.

She knew he was a good man, and someone she could fall in love with, but what about Lord Haughton? Was it possible for him to care about her? Could he find a way to love her? These questions flittered through her mind as she continued to peek in his direction, heart and stomach fluttering in tandem over the possibilities.

When Lord Haughton helped her from the horse, she had to remind herself to breathe. Although he wore gloves, from his touch she'd convinced herself he was the only man worth knowing. *How can I be so smitten? He is a new acquaintance. I am acting the fool.* "Thank you, my lord."

"Tell me, Lady Charlotte, how long have you worked to perfect your talent of painting?"

"A long time now, since I was a child. It has been a challenge and a joy to learn, as I was not a natural."

"I do not know of many people who are naturals. It takes work to be successful."

"Yes indeed." *I am making a ninny of myself.* She found a place to set her easel and a central tree for her canvas. Collin rushed to help her with the items before Haughton could offer. Ignoring the annoyed smolder on Collin's face, she turned back to Haughton. "How long have you been painting?"

"My mother hired a tutor to train me on acrylics. I learned from the age of five."

"So long? Do you have any masterpieces to display?"

Lord Haughton laughed. "Only my mother views them as masterpieces. Anyone else would see them as something an amateur would produce."

"I believe it is a mother's duty to dote on her children's accomplishments."

"And my mother does so openly and without shame," he teased.

Charlotte loved his mannerisms. She found she loved everything about the man. But how to get him to propose, she knew not. *How can I already be thinking about a proposal? I just met him. I wish my mother had never spoke of Ashby's plans for my future.* Ashby's possible ulterior motives were causing Charlotte to make much more of the outing than it was supposed to be. Lord Haughton was kind and joining her in this activity was for friendly companionship.

The morning moved into late afternoon as they spoke about color, light, shading, and brush strokes. He was, in her estimation, a kindred spirit. Taking deep breaths each time her heart sped up in hope of a relationship building, Charlotte participated in a great deal of talking to herself. She reminded her foolish brain to stop making up scenarios that would never happen. Each time she talked herself out of a possible future with this man, a sadness crept in, leaving her solemn.

"May I see your canvas?" she asked with far too much curiosity.

"If I am allowed to view yours."

"Certainly!" Surprised he'd ask, she moved away from her canvas. It was not her best work, as she'd been distracted during the creation, but there was no embarrassment in showing him.

He looked at it with a critical eye of one who knew artwork. "It is lovely." His words echoed through her head as she considered what he said. Is he trying to find something nice to say? She looked back at her painting and moved in front of it.

"Is this your only response?" she asked, giving him a teasing smile.

He tilted his head as he considered his next words carefully. "I like the liberty you took with the trees."

Again, another statement which could be construed many ways. "Did you like the brush strokes?"

"Yes, I can see the strength behind them." He lifted her paint brush and smoothed one of the lines. "Forgive me, but it did not lay right on the canvas."

She stood and looked at him as he'd looked at her canvas. Without saying a word, she took one of her paintbrushes and before she could stop herself, she ran the brush across his cheek. Blue paint smeared from his nose to his ear. "Forgive me, but it seemed as though the line was not right on the canvas."

"You did not paint my face?" His mouth turned up in a mischievous smile. Relief went through her as she realized he enjoyed her playful flirting. He walked toward her with a brush full of yellow paint.

"Do not act on your current thought!" Charlotte said backing away from him. "It would be very ungentlemanly of you."

Raising his eyebrows in surprise, he stopped walking as though he needed to think of a response. "And what would you consider your actions?"

"A momentary lapse in propriety. . ." She cringed as the words came out, hoping he would agree and leave her without paint.

"Ah . . . well . . . if you are allowed such liberties, I have only to repay you in kind."

Charlotte giggled. Then covered her mouth as she didn't mean to allow such a silly response to his words. Taking a moment to recover, she cleared her throat and stood with decorum. "I am a bit tired. I think I will go home."

He took hold of her arm to try and stop her from leaving. "Please do not go." Before she could reply he brought the paintbrush up and ran it over her nose.

Nervous, as she'd been the one to start the paint war, Charlotte looked into his eyes. Would he kiss her? She wanted him to. She wanted to keep the flirtation going. Instead, propriety overcame her thoughts. "I should return to Wentworth Hall to assist my mother with the rest of the guests."

He raised his brush and painted her chin. "Each time you claim you must leave, I will find another place to paint."

"You would not dare!" Although she made her tone disagreeable, she wanted him to continue to flirt with her. If he rubbed the paint across her face, she would not mind.

"Lady Charlotte, I am of a very serious nature. I do dare." The serious tone he used sent her back into laughter.

She backed away from him with the intent of gathering her paint supplies. He took it as a flirtatious move, and they ended up with more paint on their faces.

"My lady," Collin's voice broke through the laughter she shared with Haughton, reminding her they were not alone.

"Yes, Collin?" She turned to look at him, as a splash of paint hit her chin. Unable to hold in the laughter, Charlotte ignored the comment from the footman and sent another splotch of paint toward Lord Haughton.

"Lord Haughton!" Collin's voice rose over their laughter with an air of superiority. "Lady Charlotte is not your canvas."

Holding in her laughter as Lord Haughton nodded to the footman, Charlotte wondered how he would handle the censure. Biting her lip and silently pleading he would treat Collin with kindness, she waited. A man who treated servants unkindly wouldn't be worth her notice.

"I apologize, Collin. I should have treated the lady with more respect."

Charlotte put her hand over her paint-ridden face in an effort to hide the smile. Lord Haughton stood as though he were a naughty child receiving a tongue lashing.

"I will make certain Duke Ashby is made aware of the treatment his daughter received at your hand."

"As he should be informed. Again, I apologize and will treat her with the respect she deserves going forward."

"No harm has been done." Charlotte didn't mind servants speaking up, but reproving Lord Haughton in this manner was inappropriate. "My father will not find this information of use. It would be better for you, Collin, to stay silent on the matter."

"My lady, I beg you understand your behavior is unbecoming for the daughter of a duke." Collin's face went red as he spoke.

Annoyed by his reproval of her behavior, Charlotte glared. "What right have you to determine how I should behave? I will thank you to gather our belongings and the horses. Lord Haughton and I will walk back to Wentworth Hall."

She didn't speak until they were away from Collin. "Please forgive his insolence. He spoke out of turn."

"I am only disturbed by his censure, as it seems to be a source of discomfort for you."

Looking to Lord Haughton, she was surprised to see a smile on his face. "Why do you laugh?"

"Lady Charlotte, I should have acted with proper decorum. We are fortunate the footman was the only witness to our escapade."

Sighing in resignation, Charlotte nodded. "I know. But it was great fun." She looked to the dirt pathway, afraid to see his reaction. "Why is it, everything fun is improper?"

When Lord Haughton gave a booming laugh, Charlotte smiled and blushed. Looking into his painted face, she saw a sparkle of pleasure that made her heart skip a beat.

"Do you think contentment can be found without such improper activities?"

"I am not certain I understand your question."

"I wonder if you would be happy in a marriage with someone less inclined to using your face as a canvas."

Charlotte bit her lips as she considered his query. "I believe people who find their soul mates do not have to be content in life."

The daring words escaped her loose tongue without thought. She'd recently read the term and thought deeply over the possibility of finding a man who fit the description. Blushing furiously, she increased her step to avoid the smirk on his face.

"This is an interesting thought. What qualities would your soul mate possess?"

"Why do you ask?"

"A man should know what is expected when attempting to court a lady."

Charlotte held up her hand to count off the qualities with each finger, inwardly smiling at the thought of being courted. "He must be kind to everyone no matter their station."

"An admirable quality. Must he be generous as well?"

She tried not to smile at his addition to her list, but found it was a good suggestion. "Yes. Generosity is very important, as is sensitivity to others and their needs."

"Are you requesting the man attend lessons from a women's finishing school? These are qualities men look for in women."

Ignoring his question, Charlotte continued. "He must be committed to me, and only me as a life partner. I will not accept a man who has a mistress." Heat rushed to her cheeks as she said the scandalous word.

Garrett cleared his throat in a tone of shock. "How very bold of you to speak of such depravity."

Continuing her list, she folded another finger into her fist. "He must love painting and outdoor pursuits like riding. My life would be extremely dull without such happy moments."

"I do not think you will have troubles finding someone to ride with. Painting might be a bit harder."

Charlotte gave him an appraising look. She'd hoped he'd find she was describing the man she saw in him, but he seemed aloof to the entire meaning of her words. This caused a momentary lapse in speaking as she wondered how to make herself plain without declaring her intentions of making a match with him.

"He will have to find a way to accept my father. Ashby is not the easiest of men to speak with."

"I think all of society is aware of Ashby's nature. Is this your entire list?"

"I have only one more quality for my soul mate to hold. He must find me to be the only woman he will ever love. This love will have to last for eternity as I am convinced soul mates will stay bonded in the hereafter."

"Is this last one not the same as the depraved comment you made on mistresses?" His tone was one of laughter. Looking in his eyes, she saw a sparkle of amusement.

"No. It is very different, my lord. There are many miserable men in society who are faithful to their wives. But they are not in love. I want both love and commitment."

"It is a hefty list. Do you think you will ever find such a man?"

"I do have hope."

"What if a proposal comes and the man meets all but one requirement?"

"I will have to evaluate his offer and make a decision from the qualities he has."

"Will you make this list available to all suitors? Will you show them the expectations before they ask for your hand?"

"You are teasing me, my lord." She glared in an effort to let him know she didn't appreciate his words but couldn't hold in her laughter as she saw the wicked smile on his face.

"I do apologize, my lady. I do think your expectations are perfect for you, and I hope you are able to find a man who can live up to them."

Charlotte didn't tell him she already had as she'd only just met him. But she knew he was the man she wanted to marry, especially since Ashby had given a time frame, and she wasn't going to marry Lord Riley.

As she left him in the hall to find his chambers and clean the paint off himself, she left for her bedchamber, heart soaring at the attempt she'd made to show him her authentic self. She decided her purple dress would be perfect for the afternoon. It was said a man could never resist a woman who catches his eyes. She planned to be the only woman he admired.

Chapter 4

$\mathcal{G}$arrett entered the parlor to see Lady Charlotte looking rather beautiful in a lavender dress. The memory of their earlier flirtation made him nervous as she smiled in his direction and his heartbeat increased. Although it would have been inappropriate to keep the paint on her face, he wished there was some visual sign of their afternoon.

"Lord Haughton, have you met Lady Ruby?" Lady Violet asked, taking his attention away from Charlotte.

He did know Ruby. She was a bit of a brat, as he recalled from years past. He'd known her since she was an awkward little girl but hadn't seen her for years due to his disinterest in London and society as a whole.

Taking his eyes off Charlotte, he turned to see Lady Violet pointing to the most beautiful woman he'd ever had the pleasure of meeting. If she was still annoying, her beauty would not matter. If she was still an unbearable brat, he would not care to speak with her. She had the lightest blond hair he'd ever seen, nearly white and her green eyes sparkled with amusement at his surprised look. When he realized he was staring, he recovered his voice. "It has been a long time since I met her last."

Forgetting his desire to speak with Charlotte, he wandered across the room. "Lady Ruby."

"Yes? Lord Haughton, I have not seen you since my first season two years ago."

"Has it really been so long?" He hoped to not make a fool out of himself as he looked at her very beautiful face. *How could I have not* seen her before now? He tried to stop staring but did not want to turn away.

"Perhaps you will come back to London after the house party is over, instead of hiding away in Cheshire." Her voice was similar to a song, causing his heart to melt.

If this is what they call love, I do not want to know heart break. Love at first sight was something he'd read about but not an emotion he thought he could experience. Remembering the word *soul mate* from his conversation with Charlotte, he realized there was a possibility he now understood the word. "Of course," he said without hesitation. He would give her anything she wanted, as long as it included spending the rest of their lives together.

Realizing he was staring, and probably looked ridiculous, Garrett turned to the rest of the women and took notice of the hurt on Charlotte's face. He had a moment of confusion. Charlotte was also beautiful, but she didn't inspire his heart to pound as if a mallet were breaking through his chest. *How can I have a desire for both of these ladies?* Confused with his emotions, he thought about asking for a private moment with Charlotte, but it would be irresponsible and would suggest a courtship, which he now wanted with Lady Ruby. Yet he also wanted something with Charlotte, *perhaps friendship?*

If he were honest with himself, he liked Charlotte. If given a chance, it could grow into love. Charlotte inspired him to be the man of her dreams, and yet how could he understand such feelings in a short time?

He'd known Ruby for years, and this was the first attraction he'd had toward her. How could this be love? To stop the pang of guilt building inside him, he decided there would be someone else for Charlotte. He would find a way to apologize and let her know he only wanted friendship, when there was not an audience.

As he walked away, the hurt expression on Charlotte's face stayed imprinted on his mind. He stayed as far from the house as he could for the rest of the day to avoid Lady Charlotte. As he met the party in the parlor before going through to dinner, he made certain to stand near Ruby so he could escort her. As she took his arm, he looked to

Charlotte to see she was walking through with Lord Joshua Madden. He let out a sigh of relief. If Madden and Charlotte made a match, his guilt would be assuaged.

Chapter 5

Ruby batted her eyes and smiled at Lord Haughton as often as she could. Her father tasked her with making a match, and she would not fail him. Haughton had always been a gentleman to her. He was handsome, well liked among the *ton*, and he had a title and a fortune. All qualities her father laid out for her as important in a future spouse.

"Lord Haughton, what brings you to this side of the room?" Ruby said with a big smile. It usually only took a few nights of talking to a man for him to fall in love with her. She'd broken a few men the last season who had designs on her fortune. But her father's words were clear, a man with a fortune. Word had not yet spread of her father's ruin.

"I thought we could continue our conversation from dinner."

Ruby smiled. *It took only an hour to get this one. Father will be proud.* "This might be an invasive question, but do you enjoy the theatre?"

"I do not believe I have given it much thought."

A wealthy man, even if she didn't love him, would be a wonderful companion if they could enjoy a night out at the theater while in London. She could imagine a marriage of friendship with Lord Haughton.

"Which theater do you prefer?" Haughton asked.

"Drury Lane is the only one I have been to, my lord."

"We must remedy your lack of experience at the theater. You plan to be in London this year?"

Ruby sighed. "Yes, I do."

"Does that not please you?"

"Oh, yes it does. I apologize, I saw something distressing." It was the only excuse she could find, as she didn't want Lord Haughton to inquire to her displeasure over Madden's approach.

"Lord Madden," Haughton said in a cordial tone, "I thought to speak with Lady Ruby alone tonight."

Madden smiled and Ruby thought her knees would go weak. She'd explained her father's expectations to Madden in a letter. He responded and told her he understood. To have him approach her at this moment was unmistakably rude and yet made her heart throb uncontrollably.

"Lord Madden," Ruby said as she nodded in his direction, "I did not know you were acquainted with the Duke and Duchess of Ashby."

"Yes, my lady, my family have been invited to the house party every year at Wentworth Hall. There is no reason for us to stay away this year."

"Of course not," Ruby said, her throat drying up as though the glass she held had sand instead of punch.

Ruby closed her eyes in embarrassment as Haughton spoke. "It seems as though I am the intruder, please forgive me."

"Lord Haughton," Ruby said regaining her composure, "I enjoyed our discussion."

"As did I, my lady." Haughton nodded to both she and Madden before stepping away.

As soon as he was out of hearing, Ruby turned to Madden. "You received my missive?"

"Yes, Ruby, I did."

"You know I cannot marry you."

"I know what you said in your letter, but I do not believe your father could be so uncaring."

"This decision has nothing to do with his thoughtlessness. My family will be financially ruined if I do not make an advantageous match."

"You believe Haughton is the man to save your family fortune?"

"If my father agrees, then yes."

Madden pointed to the patio and left. Ruby waited and looked around the room to make certain no one was watching before she followed him. She loved Joshua Madden but being the younger son, he did not have the inheritance needed for her father to recover from the poor investments he'd made.

Meeting him in the alcove, Ruby wanted to leave him with the knowledge of her duty, but when they were alone, she allowed him to pull her into his arms.

"I have missed you, my love." Madden's voice sent shivers of pleasure through her body.

She allowed the excitement to course through her, and then had to stop dreaming as she remembered her father's edict. Pulling away from him, she turned toward the wall. "We cannot continue on this way."

"Run away with me. Gretna Green is a short ride from here. Your father will not notice we have left if we go while he is hunting."

Turning back toward the man she loved, Ruby wondered if he realized what he'd said. "You would have me leave my family in ruin?"

"No." She could see his effort at backtracking as he spluttered out apologies. Not a word brought her joy, as the situation was hopeless. "No, my love. But nor would I have you marry anyone other than me."

"My father would have me disowned if I do not make the match he requires. I cannot lose my family." If she didn't have to worry about her brother, mother, and father, she'd run away with Madden that very moment. But, no matter her father's faults, she loved him.

Ruby allowed Madden to hold her and kiss her as they hid in a garden alcove. If her father knew, if anyone knew what she was doing, she'd be ruined. The entire charade of finding a wealthy husband would be over. Again she'd be ostracized from her family and everything she knew.

Chapter 6

Charlotte berated herself for flirting with Lord Haughton while painting. If she hadn't been so quick to further their acquaintance, he might have kept his eyes in his head when he was introduced to Lady Ruby. She'd frightened him with her forward behavior and the list of qualities for a soul mate.

Supper with Lord Madden was nice, but he wasn't Lord Houghton and she didn't feel a connection to him. He might fulfill some of the requirements of a soul mate, but she didn't know if she could love him. He slurped his soup, which set her nerves on end.

After supper, she looked around to make certain no one would miss her, then slipped out to the stables. Tired of company, Charlotte wanted to visit her horse so she could be as far away from Ruby and Lord Haughton as she could without being visibly rude. Charlotte stood next to Magenta's stall, brushing the horse down. Magenta didn't need the grooming, as the staff took excellent care of the horses, but it was something to do and it was a way to bond with the horse.

"I wondered where you had gone off to."

Charlotte cringed as she recognized the voice. "Lord Riley, I needed a moment of solitude."

"Surprisingly, so did I."

I doubt that, she thought. He stepped into the stall, making himself comfortable as he leaned against the walls.

"These stalls are extraordinarily private." Riley examined the area with a malevolent smile on his face.

"My father had the stables rebuilt a few years ago. He wanted it to be the envy of everyone who visited." Never had this thought been so pleasant as it was at that moment. Charlotte saw the jealousy in Riley's face.

"Ashby has beautiful things," Lord Riley said turning from the horse to look at Charlotte. "I do not only mean this edifice. I have come prepared to admire you and your sister."

Stepping back from him, Charlotte held her breath, unable to form a response. She didn't want him to admire her and Marianne would be angry to think Riley had any intentions toward her as well.

"When I admire a woman, I desire a show of willingness from her."

Charlotte took another step away from him, bumping into the back of the stall. "Lord Riley, I have no desire to be admired by you."

"You will." His toothy grin made her feel dirty as he reached out and wrapped his fingers in her loose curls.

"Do not touch me. My father is a duke. He will have you punished if you injure me."

"All will be made right with a marriage. Duchess Ashby invited the local vicar, we can wed tonight."

Charlotte hit his hand away as his finger's slowly caressed her cheek. "Stay away from me."

"Ashby gave me permission. He was right, he does have beautiful daughters."

"Yes, he does." Lord Haughton's voice came from the opening of the stall. "Arundel, would you agree with Lord Riley?"

Charlotte gave a visible sigh of relief as Riley stepped away from her.

"Ashby has high expectations," Arundel responded, "Lord Riley, I believe the party is in the parlor this evening."

"I stepped out for a bit of air, Lord Arundel."

"Thankfully, so did we." Arundel's smile did not reach his eyes. "Lord Riley, neither of my sisters want or appreciate your attentions. I will also make certain Ashby expresses this sentiment to you as well."

Arundel and Haughton stared him down until he left the barn, and, without warning, Charlotte broke down in tears. She'd never experienced fear from a man advancing on her. Rushing into Arundel's arms, she didn't care if Haughton saw her cry. Too upset about the situation, embarrassment was not in her thoughts.

"It is as Mother and I feared. Ashby invited Riley here for marital purposes." Arundel rubbed her back while she cried in his arms. "I will speak with him. Stop this match from progressing."

"I was so frightened." Charlotte sniffled, accepting Arundel's handkerchief.

"I will keep an eye out for Riley." Arundel's words were supposed to bring comfort, but they didn't. Her father would give her away to a rake to forward his social standing. Ashby was wealthy and revered by many in society. He did not need the help. As one of the wealthiest dukes, Ashby had no need for more money or prestige, yet he constantly sought the means to increase his wealth. Lord Riley would be the perfect idiot to help Ashby with the process.

"Should we return to the party?" Haughton asked. She'd forgotten he was there. His soft, sympathetic tone sent a wave of longing and sadness through her.

Turning away so he couldn't see her red face, she shook her head. "No, I am finished for the evening. Phillip, will you walk me to my room? Thank you for your assistance, Lord Haughton."

She gave a quick curtsy in his direction, ashamed of her tears. She wished she had stayed inside instead of making herself a target for Lord Riley. As she prepared for bed, she worried Haughton would never consider her for a match. She not only had to contend with Ruby, but she had to fight off a predator. Haughton would find less dramatics with Ruby.

After a sleepless night, Charlotte made her way to the barn. Her mind drifted to Riley and his inappropriate advances, then switched to Lord Haughton and his admiration for Ruby. Both scenarios tortured her soul. In an effort to rid her mind of the constant worry of what would happen, Charlotte wandered out to the stables for her morning ride.

"My lady," Collin said as he held the door open for her.

"Thank you, Collin." She nodded in his direction, as she always did to each servant.

"May I speak with you?" Collin asked, walking next to her. It was unusual, but she did not mind.

"Can I help you with something?"

Without preamble, Collin spoke with a brotherly concern. "I wanted to warn you to stay away from Lord Haughton. I do not trust the man."

Surprised by his comment, Charlotte stopped and turned toward him. "What do you mean?"

"He puts on airs, and I do not trust him."

"He is an earl. He has the right to put on airs, but I have never seen such behavior from him."

"Do my observations mean nothing to you?"

Taken aback by his abrupt change from a caring brother to an over-protective friend, Charlotte backed away from him. "Has he given you cause to distrust him?"

"Yes."

"Then please, tell me what he has done."

"I cannot. It is not one instance. Since he arrived at Wentworth Hall, I have found myself in constant worry over you."

"You tell me you do not trust him but give me no reason for it. I find Lord Haughton to be the best of men. The only better I have found are my brothers." She didn't want to sound rude, but there was no reason for his concern. "Collin, I have more than enough brothers. You are a hired footman and have no need to concern yourself over me. Lord Arundel and my two other brothers take great efforts to keep me out of danger."

Collin grunted. "I knew you would not trust me."

Charlotte walked again toward the stables. "Collin. It is not a matter of trust. It is a matter of your lack of information. If you could give me a reason as to why you feel this way, I might be able to understand. Now, if you will excuse me, I plan to go for a ride." Stepping into the barn, she left Collin gaping at the door. He'd never been so forward, and it bothered her he thought it was appropriate to speak in such a way and so negatively of Lord Haughton.

Magenta stood where she'd left her the night before. Charlotte waited for the groom to saddle her horse. Caught up in the memory of Lord Riley's words and intentions, she stepped into the stall and stared at the wall. *If Phillip and Haughton hadn't followed Riley out . . .* Letting her mind dwell on what could have been only caused more distress. Charlotte turned to leave and take her thoughts on a ride as she noticed Lord Haughton standing behind her.

Startled by his approach, she found it a pleasant surprise. With the little sleep she'd had the night before, she was happy to see him. "Lord Haughton, I did not expect to see anyone out so early."

"I apologize for startling you."

She held a hand up to let him know there wasn't any reason to apologize. His tall handsome features took the air from her lungs as she remembered her tortured dreams from the night before. In these nightmares, he married Lady Ruby, leaving Charlotte to become a spinster.

"I worried when you stayed in the stall. The groom took your horse out a few minutes ago. Is something wrong?"

Charlotte turned back to the distracting wall. "I did not sleep well last night, and—" The door to the stall slammed shut, cutting off her response. Charlotte turned to see Haughton moving toward the stall door. "There is no way to open it from the inside. My father meant to have the latches fixed."

"Is it normal for the doors to swing shut?" Haughton looked unnerved by the event.

"No. But it has happened before. The groom will look for me when I do not go out directly to mount Magenta. We will not be in here long."

"I am not worried about the time, my lady."

He didn't need to finish the thought. Charlotte knew exactly where his mind had gone. If they were caught in the stall together, the innocent situation would be taken as a scandal. "I am sorry, Lord Haughton. I believe you would rather be in here with Lady Ruby."

"No, I would not."

She wondered at his quick response and the determined look on his face but didn't ask. It was not any of her business, yet something told her he wasn't as enamored with Ruby as he had been the night before.

Taking a seat on the ground, as there was not a bench or even a bucket to sit upon, Charlotte pointed to the other side of the stall. "Perhaps if you stay over there, you will not worry about a scandal."

"Who said anything about a scandal?"

"You did, with your eyes and tense posture."

Haughton moved to the spot she'd indicated and sat. "I apologize."

"Is it so terrible to think of being stuck with me?" She tried not to sound hurt, but it was nearly impossible as she was emotionally distraught over the previous evening to where her mind wouldn't allow her to rest. She had laid staring at the ceiling for the majority of the night.

Haughton took a visibly deep breath before responding. "I do not care to be caught in a scandal with you or any other lady. I know this might sound crazy, but I agree with what you were speaking of yesterday. I also hope to find a soul mate."

With this information, the exhaustion left Charlotte's mind. She wanted to know everything about Lord Haughton's hope for a wife. "Do you have specific qualities you hope for in this soul mate?"

"No. I have not taken thought for such things."

"We have time now. What would you hope for in a future soul mate?"

"We are not having a discussion such as this. I refuse to speak of such things around a lady."

"It is not inappropriate." She twisted her fingers around a loose thread in her riding habit. She'd asked her maid, Molly, to fix the seam, but it hadn't been repaired and if Charlotte continued to play with the thread, it might come undone.

Haughton shook his head. "I will not speak of such things. You will have to find a different topic of conversation."

"Do you smell that?" Charlotte's nose scrunched up as her mind registered the smell of smoke.

"It is a bit chilly this morning. There was a fire in the yard for the servants. I saw it when I came in." Haughton looked confident in his assessment, and so Charlotte nodded and hoped to think of something else to speak of.

"Would you like to play a game?" Charlotte gave a hopeful smile and saw Haughton's resolve to remain distant crumble.

"Do you have one in mind?"

"Yes, have you ever played the guessing game?"

"Guessing riddles?"

"No. I will find an object in this area and describe it. You will have to make a guess of what I am speaking of. You have only five chances before I win."

"There is not much to choose from in here. I suppose it will not hurt to play."

Determined to win each round, Charlotte looked around the stall until she found a tiny blade of grass. "This object is thin, green, and usually found outdoors. There is only one of this object in the stall."

"Are you in earnest?" Haughton's disgust was evident on his face. "How do you suppose I guess what you are referring to with such a vague description?"

Annoyed at his negative attitude, Charlotte turned her head away from him. "If you can do better, you find an object to describe."

"I can do much better." Haughton looked around the stall, then stared directly into her eyes as he spoke. Her heart raced with the description. "Red, like a rose blooming on a beautiful spring morning. A small dip in the top. What am I describing?"

Charlotte composed her shock as she looked around the stall. There wasn't a single red item anywhere. "This item must be in your imagination, my lord. I do not see anything to match the description."

Haughton smiled as he continued his penetrating gaze. She wanted to tell him to look away and yet feared he would.

"It is a very real item, and it is in this stall."

Feeling the heat rise in her cheeks, she wondered if he could be speaking of her blush. "Do not make sport out of my embarrassment."

"I would never do such a thing."

"I cannot think of what this object could be."

Charlotte's eyes went wide as Haughton moved next to her. He raised his eyebrows and smiled in a show of winning the game. "It is your lips."

Standing to move away from him, Charlotte's blush burned. "Lord Haughton, how very inappropriate of you."

"I apologize, you are correct, and I should never have suggested your lips are red as a rose."

Unable to stop herself from falling into his handsome gaze, Charlotte decided in that moment she wanted nothing more than to kiss him. As the thought passed through her mind, she stepped forward, went up on the tips of her toes, and placed a kiss on his lips. As this was her first experience with kissing, she didn't know what to expect.

Chapter 7

When he chose her lips as the item to describe, he didn't expect to receive a kiss in return. Charlotte's soft lips molded to his as though they were made to press against each other. He responded immediately, as a rush of emotions and desire spread through him. He wanted to stay in the moment forever, placing short, sweet kisses on her lips, then switching to a long deep meaningful expression of desire.

But, what would a kiss and passion say to Charlotte? What was he communicating to her as he participated in this moment? He wanted to love her, but he didn't find her as attractive as Ruby. He enjoyed her playful personality and her ability to be wise and serious when needed. He saw her loyalty to family. But what about Ruby?

His mind registered a frenzy of noise from outside the stall as he ran his hand down her back and pushed concern aside. Caught up in the passion of kissing, he ignored the desire to find out what could cause such a loud commotion, until the smell of smoke filled his intake of breath. Garrett pulled away from the embrace and looked at Charlotte for a second before reacting to the sounds outside of the stall.

Pounding on the stall door, Garrett yelled for assistance. "We are stuck in here. Please open the door."

Ashamed of his scandalous behavior with Charlotte only a moment before, he continued to pound on the door hoping someone would hear. Avoiding any glance in her direction, Garrett wondered at the pleasure and perfection he'd experienced. He'd kissed other women, but never with so much vigor. The mere thought of Charlotte made him want to abandon the door to continue kissing her, but the smoke filling their stall forced him to push thoughts of passion out of his mind.

"Let us out." Charlotte's perfectly feminine cry pierced the air around them but didn't bring anyone to their rescue.

Coughing from the smoke seeping into every crevice, Garrett knew they had to find a way out of the stall. The barn had to be on fire.

"Charlotte, stand back."

"What are you going to do?"

"I will try to run and boost myself over the stall door." If Ashby hadn't been so keen to outwit every other duke, earl, marquess, and possibly the king, this wouldn't be a problem. But the man had a penchant for perfection and expecting the best. His stables would have to be amazing and near impossible to escape.

Garrett stood at the back of the stall and ran the few feet jumping at the last minute. His hands grabbed hold of the top of the door, and, to his surprise, Charlotte took hold of his feet, boosting him up. The smoke at the top was thicker than below, breathing in filled his throat with the itchy dry stench. Coughing, he had to remember to open the stall door as he dropped to the ground.

Doubled over as he tried to breathe, Garrett removed his cravat and covered his mouth. The latch on the stall door was suspiciously locked, but he didn't take the time to examine the reasons. As the door swung open, he pulled Charlotte into his embrace, handed her his cravat and they ran to the exit.

He watched as Charlotte was taken up to her chambers. Coughing to clear his lungs, he stood in the duke's den waiting for the questions. His hands shook from the adrenaline of the stressful situation. Unable to calm his nerves, he accepted a glass of water from the butler, and then a stronger drink from Ashby.

The smooth liquid poured down his throat. He didn't drink often but knew it would help calm the shaking in his hands. Placing the glass on the table, he waited for the interview.

"Lord Haughton, I would be a very ungrateful man if I did not thank you for saving my daughter's life." Ashby's towering frame seemed larger as he stood over Garrett's seated position.

He wanted to respond but didn't know how, so he stayed silent.

"Will you tell us what happened?"

"Give him time to rest, be checked out by a physician, and get control of his anxiety." His father's voice boomed over Ashby's question.

"If he relays the information now, by the time the physician is finished with Charlotte, he will be able to administer to Haughton." Duke Dudley's response surprised Garrett, as he hadn't notice him in the room.

Taking a brief scan of the people surrounding him, he noticed it was only Ashby, Dudley, and Cholmondeley. If he gave the whole of the story, it would compromise both he and Charlotte. Feeling there wasn't another option, as he was worn out, he decided the truth was the right way to go. Remembering the way Ruby looked at Lord Madden the night before, Garrett relayed the entire story. As he finished, he looked to Duke Ashby. "I will ask for Charlotte's hand, your grace."

Dudley cleared his throat. "I do not think such an action is necessary. What do you think, Cholmondeley?"

His father patted him on the shoulder. "I think you should see a physician before any decisions are made."

"This younger generation is known for stealing kisses in gardens. A stable is similar." Dudley spoke as though an authority on the matter.

Garrett looked at Ashby to see he was glaring at Dudley. Silence from the duke sent a shiver through his already trembling body.

Ashby fisted his hands, an outward sign of controlling his anger. "Haughton, I will have the doctor visit your chambers. You should do as your father suggests, rest."

The cool collected tone was at odds with the anger piercing Ashby's face. Knowing he was dismissed, Garrett stood and rushed from the room.

He didn't consider himself a hero, but by the time he woke, and the doctor cleared him for normal activities, Ruby made him out to be one.

"I cannot imagine how frightening it had to be fighting to escape a burning structure as you did." She batted her eyes and touched his arm in a very seductive way. He appreciated her attentions and ignored the nagging in his gut telling him she wasn't sincere. He'd seen the way she looked at Madden. He also remembered the kiss he'd shared with Charlotte. It had been perfect. Why was she now flattering him?

If Ruby were to be believed, he was courageous, reckless, and yet heroic. He remembered the fear of smoke invading his lungs and the worry that they wouldn't escape. And with each thought of Charlotte, a wave of guilt and passion followed.

"Haughton, are you listening to me?" Ruby's voice rang through his ears. He turned toward her, as she asked him to walk with her through the gardens.

The end of summer breeze was perfect, and he was sharing it with a very beautiful woman who was pouting as he missed her words. Her lips were very plush, pressed together with a soft look of pain. His silence had hurt her feelings.

"I apologize, Ruby. What were you speaking of?"

"I wanted to know if there is information on how the fire started?"

Shaking his head, he looked over to where the burned-out building sat. The horses were tethered in the stable yard. "I do not think Ashby has any idea. The most common discussion is a spark ignited hay from the fire they had in the yard."

"I have nightmares of the entire event. When I saw you running with Lady Charlotte out of the stables, I realized I could have lost you."

Garrett looked into her beautiful emerald eyes as they sparkled in the sun. She was in earnest. Had he imagined the longing in her eyes when speaking with Madden? "I am fine."

"Your voice is raspy. I will not rest until you do not sound as though you are ailing. I think you should spend the day in bed."

He wanted to ask about Lord Madden as he listened to her concern for his welfare. Perhaps he'd been under the wrong impression and Ruby wasn't taken with Madden. He was confused with his feelings. The connection he'd made with Charlotte was passionate and felt right, but he also had a connection with Ruby, and she somehow managed to muddle every romantic thought he had toward any other woman.

Chapter 8

Charlotte spent far too much time preparing for the moment Lord Haughton would see her standing across the room. She had yet to see him since the fire and their kiss. From their time together, she assumed he held her in the same regard she had for him. She'd built it up in her mind while resting from the incident in the barn. Replayed the kiss over and over. Not only was it his duty to marry her after such a passionate moment, but she was convinced he wanted to marry her.

She hoped Haughton would ask her to dance more than once. And she wanted him to ask for the supper dance, which would then mean they would be seated together during the meal. She hoped to steal away into the gardens after supper to thank him for saving her life and to let him steal another kiss. It was all she could think of anymore. She only hoped a blush wouldn't accompany any part of the evening.

"You look beautiful," Emma said as she sidled up against her.

"Thank you. I asked Molly to set my hair a little differently tonight, and I think it looks fine. Molly also scrubbed it until it no longer smelled of smoke." Charlotte gave a distressed smile. It'd taken a week of scrubbing to get rid of the stench. "And, I hope someone takes notice of me tonight."

"If he does not notice, he is not worth your time."

Charlotte shook her head. She did not agree. "Lord Haughton is everything I want in my future." Clamping her mouth shut, she realized it hadn't taken much to get her to confide. *My mind is frazzled.*

"Lord Haughton?" Emma asked in surprise and concern evident in her face. "Lottie, did you not know he is pursuing Lady Ruby?"

Pulling Emma to the side where they could talk without notice, Charlotte wanted her sister-in-law to understand. "When you knew Phillip was intended for Lady Olivia did you give up?"

"Not at first— but there was a point I did let him go— I had to. It hurt far too much to keep hoping."

"I will not give up until he is engaged."

"Lottie," Emma said, taking hold of her arm, "I know he saved your life, but I do not want to see you hurt. There are other men here. Men who are worth your notice."

Looking down at her hands, Charlotte kept her voice even as she claimed, "Lord Haughton is above all of them in kindness and compassion. I know it is silly, but I believe he is the only man I could love."

Charlotte looked up to see Lord Haughton was already in the ballroom. Unfortunately, speaking with Lady Ruby. She looked back at Emma. "I need to do something to get rid of Ruby. Perhaps send an urgent missive to her father making up some dreadful news from their estate?"

Emma laughed, "I will do my best to feign surprise."

"Nothing is final until an engagement is made," Charlotte said with a playful wag of her eyebrows. "I plan to make certain the engagement is with me."

"I pray you are successful. Ruby seems to have a strange effect on the men in this room."

The statement was true. Men flocked to Ruby and tripped over each other to dance and speak to her.

Entering the ballroom, Charlotte did not have to wait long to be asked for a dance, Lord Madden moved to her side with haste.

"Lady Charlotte, I wondered if you were still unwell due to your delayed arrival."

"I am much recovered, Lord Madden, there was no need to worry. The dancing has not even begun. I have only missed a few moments of socializing."

"As I can now see. You do look majestic this evening."

"Thank you." Charlotte gave him a kind smile, but hoped it was plain enough not to encourage him. She was interested in one man and vowed to do her all to get his attention on her.

"Will you join me for the first dance?"

"Yes, thank you for the offer."

Lord Madden nodded and moved away to secure more partners for the evening. Charlotte locked eyes and smiled at Marianne as they both noticed he headed straight to her. Marianne did not find Madden handsome or genuine. Charlotte held in her laughter as she watched Marianne accept an invitation.

"Lady Charlotte, will you bring me into your confidence?"

Charlotte turned to see Haughton next to her. Instantly smiling, she loved the brightness and effect of his presence. He made her happy. "What would you like to know, my lord?"

"I want to know what has caused your mouth to turn up in joy and your eyes to sparkle."

Telling him the sparkle in her eyes was due to his presence would make her a fool. "Tell me Lord Haughton, what do you think is the cause?"

"One would think Lord Madden's offer of a dance was the reason for your excitement."

"Certainly not!" Charlotte said without thought. Recovering from her surprise, she backtracked. "I . . . I . . . mean, yes he did ask me for a dance, but I feel the same about his offer as I would any offer." *Lovely, I have just told him I have no favor toward him.*

Lord Haughton smiled at her. "Thank you for your confession. I hoped this was the case."

"What do you mean?"

"I would like to ask you for the supper dance."

"You would?" she questioned looking toward Lady Ruby in surprise. Her devious plan was in motion and she had only to convince him of his love for her before the night was through.

"Yes, but as a friend."

"There is no need to clarify, Lord Haughton. Of course, I see you as a friend."

He nervously looked toward Lady Ruby then back to Charlotte. "I did not secure Lady Ruby's supper dance. Lord Farland asked before I was able to do so."

Realizing she was the second choice for his offering, she gave him her biggest smile and pushed aside the hurt. "I would love to join you for the supper dance, my lord."

"Thank you for understanding. Also, while I am here, I would like to apologize for painting your face last week, and for our—" She held her hands up as the kiss they'd shared was not meant for anyone to overhear.

"My actions were not those of a gentleman."

Thrown off guard, Charlotte nodded her acceptance of the apology. She'd all but forgotten the stolen moments in the meadow but relived the kiss and his embrace over and over since it'd happened.

He held his arm out for her and guided her to the refreshment table. "Will you confide in me. Tell me your secrets and reveal to me what was so amusing when I found you?"

Deciding it would not hurt, as he wanted to be her friend, she admitted, "Marianne does not appreciate Lord Madden's attentions toward her."

"He is a bit of a fop," Lord Haughton said while handing her a glass of punch.

"Yes, but despite his ridiculous behavior, he is a kind man."

"Very true, Madden was at Eton with your brothers and me. He is a good man, despite his desire to bring humor to every situation." He paused for a moment before asking, "Tell me, Lady Charlotte, what is your impression of Lady Ruby?"

Not knowing her well enough, Charlotte could not give a decent assessment. "She seems like a very good sort of girl. This is the first I have met her. My father and Duke Dudley became friends after the debacle with Duke Norland last season. Dudley has been a calming influence on my father, and he does not gamble as Norland did."

"What do you mean?"

Without thought, she continued to talk. "My father enjoyed high stake gambling with the Duke of Norland. After the broken engagement last year, they have decided to take a break in their friendship." Charlotte put her hand over her mouth as she realized what she was saying. "I do apologize for speaking so plainly, my lord."

"No need to apologize."

"Please do not mention this to anyone."

"I did ask you to take me into your confidence, my lady."

"Yes . . ." Her words trailed off as she thought of her father's reaction if he knew what she'd said. Her father, the Duke of Ashby, was known for his temper throughout the *ton*. "But I should not have spoken about such things."

"Do not worry, my lady. Your words are safe with me."

As she looked into his eyes, she knew she could trust him. "Thank you." Losing herself in his kindness, she did not realize the dancing was ready to begin until Lord Madden claimed her for the promised dance.

Lord Madden's flamboyant clothing and actions dimmed the excitement for the evening. But as promised, she danced with him.

"Lady Charlotte, please tell me how to earn favor from your sister Marianne."

Surprised by his request, she playfully asked, "What is this? You have the desire to court my sister?"

"I find she is the least objectionable of the unattached women in the room."

Not amusing! Charlotte stopped dancing. "Pardon me?"

"Come now, Lady Charlotte, you would not expect me to realize your attentions are paid elsewhere?" He nodded his head toward Lord Haughton who was dancing with Lady Ruby. "He is blind if he does not notice you."

"Sir, I do not know what you mean." Taking his hand again, she danced through to the end of the song. He did not speak again until he left her by her mother and sister.

"Thank you for the dance, my lady." He took Marianne for the next and left Charlotte to think about his comments.

She had only a moment before Lord Riley approached. "Lady Charlotte, you are quite beautiful this evening."

She did not move to give him her hand, although he reached out as though he expected her to give into his request. "Lord Riley, thank you for the compliment."

"Come now, my lady, you will not cause a scandal by denying a man when he is asking you to dance?" His toothy salacious grin sent a cold chill down her spine.

"I never once heard you make the request, my lord." Turning to her mother, she noticed the duchess was involved in a conversation and therefore not paying attention.

"Will you join me for a dance?"

"I am afraid I already claimed this one." Charlotte gave a sigh of relief as her brother Charles approached. "I apologize, Lottie, I was caught up in the other room and nearly forgot about our dance."

"Not a problem, Charles. Thank you for remembering." Taking his arm, she walked out to join the other couples and tried to ignore the glare Riley sent in her direction.

Charlotte hid her smile as Phillip and Edward moved toward Riley. The cold fear he'd caused in her moments before filled with the warmth of her brothers show of protection.

Chapter 9

With the dinner dance next, Garrett approached Charlotte and led her out to the floor. He didn't know what dance to expect but was very surprised to find it was a waltz. "How scandalous," he whispered as he put his hand on her lower back and pulled her close. "I never thought I'd see the day where the Duke of Ashby allowed a waltz to be played at his home."

He smiled as Charlotte laughed at his joke. "You do not seem to have trouble with the steps, my lord. This must mean you have danced the waltz before tonight."

"As have you, my lady." He enjoyed the sparkle in her eyes. Speaking to Charlotte was comfortable. It was much different than the conversation with Ruby where his hands would go cold and a strange sweat would break out, making him look the fool.

"I will admit to nothing, my lord." She gave him a beautiful smile. Although it was not intoxicating, as Ruby's would be, it was pleasurable to receive such a favor from her.

"Tell me, Lady Charlotte, do you have any other pursuits outside of painting?"

"Painting is my favorite past time, but I do enjoy sketching. Lady Arundel has taught me much about the art since she married Phillip."

"They seem happy, which is a feat considering the trauma of their courtship."

"They overcame the trial by not speaking about it. It is much easier for them to live in the moment and look forward to the future."

Garrett internally groaned. This was not the conversation he wanted to have with Charlotte. With the thought, he looked away to find something else to talk about when he noticed the glare he received from Lord Riley. Without thought, he asked, "Has Riley tried to speak with you again?"

"Are we going to speak of such unpleasant things, my lord?"

He laughed, "No, we should stay on pleasant ground."

"Tell me, my lord, do you enjoy reading?"

He spoke of books with her for the rest of the dance. It was rather comforting to think she wasn't trying to convince him to marry her, even after their passionate moment. The entire conversation with Ruby over the last few days was fully focused on who she would marry. Charlotte was calm and seemed to be happy with her life. He focused on the dance, as he led her around the room. It wasn't a full ballroom, which helped to keep the dance moving at a regular pace. As the song ended, he held his arm out and escorted her to dinner.

"Lord Haughton, may I ask what you enjoy doing outside of painting?"

"My favorite way to spend time is to ride through the countryside. Even when it is cold and snow is on the ground, I prefer a ride to sitting in front of a fire."

He helped her with her chair. Lady Charlotte was comfortable to him. He was not nervous and flirting with her was easy, and she was very receptive. *Why do I not care for her as I do Ruby?*

"Do you enjoy house parties?" He asked during the soup course. As she started to answer, Ruby laughed from the other end of the table, and Garrett's mind wandered. He did not hear Charlotte's reply, which made it difficult to ask the follow up question he had in mind.

"I apologize, my lady. I was distracted for a moment."

"It is quite all right, my lord. I do enjoy the company, but I think house parties are very much like London. It is easy to become exhausted."

Ruby laughed again. Garrett looked over to see her hand was on Lord Madden's arm as she had touched him earlier. *Is Ruby a flirt? She is with Madden again. What happened to Farland?*

Turning back to his conversation with Charlotte he forgot where they'd left off. Looking into her eyes, he remembered the moment before she'd gone up on her toes and placed the kiss on his lips. A rush of excitement went through him, and then fear as his mind flashed back to the fire. The room turned cold in his mind as his hand shook.

"Are you unwell?" Charlotte's question had him shaking his head to clear the memory.

He nearly responded when Ruby's voice entered his mind as he heard her flirting with Madden. It was very distracting. A part of him wanted to give up on Ruby and focus solely on Charlotte, but her mesmerizing eyes tore at his heart and he decided to continue to make a goal of winning Ruby. He excused her actions by convincing himself Ruby was flirting with Madden as he was with Charlotte. It was part of the game they played in society.

As soon as supper finished, Garrett found Ruby and asked her to take a walk. Duchess Ashby put candles and lanterns in the garden so couples could escape into the night air.

"Lord Haughton, I have to admit I am surprised you asked me to walk with you." Lady Ruby's voice chimed in the dark night sky. The stars staring down at them made for a perfect evening.

"You doubt my pursuit of you?" *What a stupid question!* he thought as he led her to an alcove. There was a spot behind the bushes where they could talk without notice.

"Very much so, especially when I see you laughing and talking with Lady Charlotte."

"I have made my intentions toward both of you clear. It is normal for a man to pursue and dance with multiple women before deciding which one to court." Although he'd made his decision, this was a concern for Garrett, Ruby was jealous of Lady Charlotte. A jealous wife would plague him far more than one who could hold her tongue.

"She is not the right woman for you, Lord Haughton. I feel as though you and I were made for each other. We are soul mates."

Fear and confusion gripped his mind as she said the word Charlotte had spent so much time thinking about. Garrett wanted to back away from Ruby and run, but she was holding his arm. Looking into her eyes, his fears dispelled. The words she'd spoken only moments ago lost in Ruby's beauty.

"I do not mean to speak negatively of her, but she will do anything to win you. If you plan to stay a bachelor, you need to stay away from her."

Garrett laughed, "Charlotte is not the type of woman you are making her out to be. She is very kind."

"Yes, but she is a spinster. She is already two and twenty. You deserve a younger woman. One who can give you an heir."

He reminded himself of the difference in conversations with Ruby and Charlotte. Ruby had come full circle to marriage, where Charlotte had never mentioned a courtship or commitment to him.

"Two and twenty is hardly old. Many women are waiting until four and twenty to marry now."

Ruby took hold of his hand and rubbed it while batting her eyes. "We should discuss something else, my lord."

He looked back into her eyes and found he wanted nothing more than to give into the desire to kiss her. Ruby was an intoxicating woman with her emerald eyes sparkling with the light from the moon. Her white-blond hair looked otherworldly as it sat piled on her head in a perfect formation of curls.

"What would you like to speak of?" he asked, recognizing the submission in his voice. Garrett's eyes went wide as she leaned toward him, her eyes closing. He'd stolen a few kisses over the years, but in the last week this was now the second woman to instigate the action. Giving into his desires, he leaned into her and covered her lips with his own. It was awkward, uncomfortable, and seemed wrong as her lips were tight with tension. *This must be a first kiss for her.* As he massaged her lips with his, she calmed and the tension left, leaving her lips soft to his touch.

As he walked her back to the ballroom, he thought about the kiss. It was nice. But it wasn't spectacular. He wondered how he could be so mesmerized by her eyes yet find very little satisfaction in physical touch. With Charlotte, the passion had spread through his entire body, requiring a fire to pull him away.

Thoughts plagued him of the dissatisfaction as he attempted to sleep. With all the kissing he'd done, none had been so disappointing as the one with Ruby. Perhaps he'd put too much pressure on the moment. Laying with closed eyes, Ruby's face appeared in his mind and he decided the discomfort had to be his worry over the jealousy. *It is normal for women to be jealous, especially where marriage is concerned.*

Chapter 10

When Lord Haughton left her to find a glass of punch, Ruby rushed out of the room. She'd only ever allowed one man to kiss her, Joshua Madden, and now Haughton. Tears fell as she realized she could never love another man. Thoughts of running away with Madden this very night played through her mind as she rushed up to her chamber and called for her maid.

"Lacy, pack a bag of clothing for me."

She spoke while searching the room for her stationary. *How can my things not be unpacked by now?* "Where is my stationary?"

"On the desk, my lady."

Ruby turned toward the writing desk and let tears flow down her face. "I am out of sorts. I apologize for getting angry with you."

"No apology needed, my lady."

Ruby ignored anything else her maid said as she wrote the letter to her parents.

Dear Mother and Father,

I cannot go through with the task you have given me. The truth is, I am deeply in love with Lord Madden. He asked me to marry him, and I believe it is the only situation in life I can bring myself to tolerate. Although love matches are frowned upon, I cannot marry for fortune. Please forgive me. Please love me even though I am a disappointment to you.

With all my love
Ruby

Sealing the folded papers with wax, Ruby handed the letter to her maid. "Please give this to my parents after I have left. Now, help me into my riding habit.

"My lady, I do not think this is a good idea." The maid stood, eyes wide in shock, the missive shaking in her hand. Ruby understood the worry. Her father was not kind to servants when receiving bad news, but she needed someone trustworthy who would deliver the note after she'd made her escape.

"My father pays you to serve me. Help me or send a different maid in who will."

"Yes, my lady."

Ruby walked to the chair by the window and sat, ready to remove her slippers when her parents entered. They walked with the grandeur of royalty.

"Mother? Father?" The guilty look on her face caused her father to point to the maid.

"Out!" he said, teeth clenched in anger.

"Ruby, Lord Haughton is looking for you. You do not have permission to be in your chambers for the night." Her father's voice shook with anger.

"I cannot do this, Father," Ruby cried looking to her mother for help. "Do not make me marry him."

Her mother shook her head to let her know a plea would not convince the duke.

"You would have our family disgraced?" Her father's fists clenched by his sides.

"I am not the one who made the poor investment." She'd wanted to say those words for so long. Now that they were out, she wanted to take them back. Her father's stunned face looked as though she'd slapped him. In a quieter voice she cried out, "I am in love with Lord Madden."

"He is a younger son. His connections will not do anything for our situation."

"Why is this my responsibility? I am not your heir."

Her brother was the heir, but he'd married years before and the dowry his wife brought to the marriage was lost in the investment.

"You know why you have been given this task. Haughton is a good man. He will treat you with kindness. If you refuse to marry him, I will find someone else. But there are few men who have the temperament of Haughton. You could end up with a difficult match."

She knew what her father meant. Her older sister was in what the family referred to as a *difficult match*. Her sister had more children than she could handle and a husband with a terribly abusive temper. Her sister Mari was lonely and depressed. Ruby did not want that for her future.

"Please, do not make me marry for convenience." Her plea fell on deaf ears.

"We will make your excuses for tonight. A headache will suffice." Her mother walked forward and put a hand on hers. Hugging her, she whispered, "If you love Madden, running away will not solve this problem. We will speak in the morning."

Her father cleared his throat with impatience. "We saw your tête-à-tête in the garden. Tomorrow you will make certain Lord Haughton understands he has proposed marriage."

Ruby looked to her father in confusion. "But he did not propose."

Raising his eyebrows, her father smiled. "You must make him believe he did."

Ruby spent the rest of the evening thinking over her mother's words, and when giving up trying to discern their meaning, she turned to plotting her escape. As she planned, she knew the escape would never happen. Frightened of what her father would do if she disobeyed, deep down the knowledge of her fate stayed with her. Madden would have to find another wife, as she would need to convince Lord Haughton of her undying love or, as her father would say, trick him into an engagement.

Chapter 11

Garrett held back from sitting next to Ruby as Charlotte was directly across from her. The thought of either lady looking at him with hurt eyes bothered him. He'd had a sleepless night thinking about the women and the kiss he'd exchanged with both. He wanted another kiss with Charlotte and wondered if another kiss with Ruby would be as disappointing as the first. Duchess Ashby asked everyone to gather in the morning room for an announcement, so he found a spot next to Edward and Phillip to await the next item on the house party agenda.

Duchess Ashby clapped her hands. "Thank you everyone for gathering here today. Before the men start discussing their hunt, I want to announce a few of our evening activities. So, please do not expend all your energies chasing animals." She gave a pointed glare to Ashby, which brought laughter to the room. "Tonight, we will have a poetry and prose reading. If you would like to participate—"

Garrett leaned closer to Edward, "Is your mother working to marry off both your sisters and Charles this year?"

Edward smirked, "Is marriage matching not the goal of every mother in this room?"

"Very true."

"Lord Haughton, thank you for volunteering," Duchess Ashby said with a mischievous smile.

Garrett smiled and nodded as though he knew what he'd just volunteered to be a part of, but he had no idea. He took the book she handed to him and looked to Phillip. "What did I just get myself into?"

"You are playing Petruchio in the performance this Saturday evening."

"Excuse me?" Acting was not one of his strengths and playing the lead male role was the last thing he wanted.

Phillip patted him on the shoulder. "Do not worry, you are not the only one in shock after being volunteered."

Garrett looked around the room to see Charlotte holding the same book he had. He raised his eyebrows at her in question and she shook her head. "I suppose I should have been listening instead of talking."

Edward and Phillip both nodded. It was hard to take either of them seriously in these types of situations.

"Come now," Duchess Ashby said trying to convince the group at large to participate, "do I have to assign everyone else?"

"Mother, neither Lottie nor Haughton volunteered for their roles. Assign the rest and let us go on our way," Edward called out, causing everyone to laugh.

With the assignments done, Garrett found his way over to Lady Charlotte. "I suppose we must practice so this is an actual performance. I would like some time to go over my lines alone though, so I can figure this out."

"Of course, my lord."

Charlotte was everything he ever wanted in a wife. When he was with her, it was easy to see her fine qualities along with her handsome features. He thought about asking for a walk in the garden, until Ruby's voice rang across the room. When he heard her voice, his mind immediately drew toward her and he did not hear what Charlotte said. It was rude, and he regretted ignoring her.

"Lord Haughton, I cannot wait to see you in the performance," Lady Ruby chimed as she took his arm.

"I do not think I will be a great performer, but I will make an effort."

Ruby looked to Lady Charlotte, "And isn't it wonderful you will play the lead female role opposite of the man who saved your life. If I had known the duchess would choose Garrett for the lead male role, I would have volunteered for Katherine."

Charlotte held the book out to her. "Please be my guest. I do not have the desire to make a spectacle of myself."

"Oh, no!" Ruby put a hand on her chest. "I would not dream of stealing your spotlight."

As Ruby walked away, Garrett turned back to Charlotte, reeling from hearing his Christian name on Ruby's intoxicating tongue. He noticed the disappointment on Charlotte's face, realized he'd been the cause of hurting her far too often of late, but instead of finding a way to apologize, he excused Ruby's jealousy. Ruby was not a catty woman. Perhaps if the duchess assigned him earlier, he'd be playing opposite Ruby. It was a matter of chance he was paired with Charlotte.

"If you'll excuse me. We will practice this afternoon?" His voice cracked as he internalized the sadness in her eyes. All thought of asking her to take a turn in the garden was pushed aside as he remembered Ruby and the sound of his Christian name escaping her mouth.

"Yes, my lord."

Although he knew he was making a fool of himself, Garrett rushed after Ruby. Perhaps she would run through the lines with him. Dancing with her the night before, he'd thought they matched in every way. He tried not to think about the kiss, as he still didn't understand the discrepancy between her lips and her eyes.

"Lady Ruby, will you walk with me?"

"Yes, my lord." The giddy smile and light laughter in her eyes pulled him toward the patio.

He led her through the garden and reveled at the touch of her hand on his arm. "Are you comfortable? Or is it too cold?" The mornings were a little chilly of late.

"Garrett," her voice came out with a sweet pout she reserved for time alone with him, I thought we were past titles after last night."

He thought about the previous night. Was it the music? The dancing? Or was it the way she looked in the low-cut red dress? It could have been all three things, but he had not expected to lose his mind and pull her in for a kiss. He'd kissed her in a very ungentlemanly way, expecting to be as mesmerized with her lips as he was with her eyes. But there seemed to be something missing. Instead of breaking away, he'd wanted to find the missing moments of the kiss. It had been inappropriate, given they were not officially courting or engaged, but he'd pressed on, kissing her cheek, neck, and behind her ear, but the attraction he'd experienced in her eyes was lost in the moment. He'd always imagined a woman sighing in pleasure when receiving kisses such as this, yet Ruby had stood motionless and still.

Stepping away from her, his hands behind his back, he said, "Yes, Ruby, I do think we can dispense with the titles."

She smiled at him, grabbed his arm, and pulled him further away from the house. He should stop her but wanted to try kissing again. Perhaps it would be different this time. First kisses were never exactly what they should be. Falling into her excitement, he pulled her to a private spot in the garden and kissed her. Surprised by her willingness, he lost himself in trying to make the kiss passionate. Starting with her lips he thought it might be better if he focused on one area instead of moving to the cheek and neck, but as he pulled away, he couldn't ignore the nagging doubt. *Was this love? What about Charlotte? Why does Ruby not respond to my kisses?* For this was the biggest issue. Ruby did not kiss him back. She let him do all the work, and never tried to increase the kiss.

"When will you speak with my father?" she asked as she wiped where he'd kissed her then looked to him and wiped her lip rouge off his lips.

"Pardon me?" Garrett looked at her, wondering how she'd misunderstood his intentions.

"Hurry, my love. I want everyone to know we are engaged. I think Duchess Ashby is trying to match you with her daughter."

"Ruby, we are not engaged."

"What do you mean?" she asked backing away from him. "You have taken liberties with me, Garrett. We are engaged."

Confused by her insistence, he backed away from her. *Have I crossed a line? Liberties?*

Ruby's eyes swam in tears. "I never would have allowed you to kiss me if I did not think you were serious in your intentions."

What did I say to make her think we are engaged? "Lady Ruby, I do not believe I asked for your hand."

Ruby's tears fell like rain from her eyes. Garrett grabbed his handkerchief and held it out for her. "I cannot believe you would be so insensitive. You have ruined me."

Eyes wide at the insinuation, Garrett rushed to pull her away from where anyone might have a chance of overhearing. "Lady Ruby, a kiss is not a reason to claim ruin. Many men steal kisses."

"I do not know what women you have spent time with, Lord Haughton, but I do not bestow such favors freely." She threw his handkerchief on the ground and ran away.

Unable to process the implications of a scandal, Garrett rushed after her. He had to stop her before she announced their argument to anyone. He had to stop her from ruining both of them.

"Lady Ruby, please wait so we can discuss this situation." Garrett called out to her as she ran further from the house.

Ruby stopped and whispered, "I do not care for your cavalier attitude toward my virtue."

"I meant no disrespect, my lady. Please understand we have had a small miscommunication." Trying for a calm and rational discussion, he pressed on. "Ruby, when we kiss, there is . . . do you enjoy it?"

Heat rushed into Ruby's face, but he had to know her answer. To be engaged and marry a woman who was not inspired by his affections would be a situation of convenience. If he wanted such a situation, his father would find a suitable match.

"Is this due to your feelings for Lady Charlotte?"

"I do not want to speak with you about Lady Charlotte." She threw Charlotte's name at him as though his conflicted feelings were wrong. He was not engaged to either woman. How could she accuse him of inappropriate behavior? Also, she deflected his question, intimating it wasn't important.

She turned from him. "What do you have to say for your actions?"

"I do not plan to be married due to a scandal. Please keep this silent. I will mind my manners in the future." His view of her changed as he saw the triumphant look in her green eyes. Eyes he thought bewitching only a few minutes before.

"You have kissed Lady Charlotte?"

"No." It was a lie. He had kissed Charlotte. He'd enjoyed it immensely. He must have looked guilty as Ruby quirked her eyebrows in disbelief.

"Make certain not to, my love. We are now engaged." Her words sounded like silk. Her voice, which only an hour before caused him to melt. Now it was a threat pouring shivers down his spine.

Fighting with her didn't resolve the misunderstanding. She left as soon as she told him they were engaged. Garrett stood in stunned silence unable to form a coherent thought as he realized she actually expected a marriage.

His discussion with Ruby should have stayed private. He took an hour to think while wondering through the garden trying to decide where he'd gone wrong. He hadn't breached the rules of etiquette. If he'd kissed her with an audience, he would be required to marry her for her reputation. But stealing a kiss in private was hardly an offense worth marriage. He could admit trying to extract passion from her was not wise, but he'd kept his hands proper. He knew men who'd done more with women and hadn't been caught by the vicar's noose, but he wasn't those men. By the time he'd returned to the house, the entire party knew about the so-called engagement.

"I am so happy. I could not keep the information to myself," Ruby said with a pout, which once would have melted his heart, spurring him toward instant forgiveness. Now he only experienced anger.

"We are not engaged, Ruby."

"Stop fighting this, my love."

"I did not ask for your hand."

"You did, when you kissed me. I am happier than I have ever been."

"I understand, but if we were to get engaged, we need to do so in the proper way. Speaking with your father for one, and he should make the announcement." Everything he said fell on deaf ears.

"Father is not one to stand on ceremony." She brushed his concerns aside rushing off to speak with her mother so wedding plans could commence.

Garrett made his way out to the stables. Angry, sick, and tired of trying to make her see reason, he needed time alone so he could think, especially if he were going to practice for a performance he did not want to put on. *Taming of the Shrew* was not one of his favorites.

The smell of burnt wood assaulted his mind as he searched for his horse. Sun Dancer stood in his makeshift stall waiting to be taken out for a ride. Garrett ignored the stable boy and saddled the horse with haste. Putting the horse into a canter, he rode through the meadow and into the woods. He'd stayed behind from the morning hunt to walk with Ruby, but suddenly wished he'd gone out with the men. Shooting a gun might make him feel better.

The wind blowing through his hair, as he'd made a conscious decision not to go up to his chambers to claim a hat, was the perfect distraction. Not a single thought of Ruby entered his mind, which was a relief as he'd been far too preoccupied by the woman.

Garrett made a zigzag through the trees, enjoying the summer breeze. It was a truly magnificent day for a ride. The sun, perfect in the sky, shone down, heating his skin and he gave a bit of a laugh as he thought of what his mother's response would be to the freckles he'd have on his nose as a prize for his joyous freedom.

Far too soon, he turned back to Wentworth Hall. Charlotte would be waiting for him as he promised to practice the play with her. With the reminder of the play, the burden of Ruby and his situation came back to him. Facing Charlotte would be much harder than the performance and in his estimation, much more difficult than trying to convince Ruby they weren't engaged.

He followed Charlotte out to the meadow, thankful for the long walk to gather his thoughts. As she turned toward him, he took a deep breath and started the apology. "I need to explain—"

Cutting him off before he could finish the sentence, Charlotte spoke over top of him. "There is no reason to apologize. Although, I have not given you my well wishes for your future."

He held his hands up to stop her joyous appraisal of his engaged status. "Please do not—"

"My lord, Lady Ruby is a wonderful woman. I have no doubt you will be happy."

Realizing she would not let him apologize and not wanting to argue with her, he held the book up and changed the topic. "We should practice." Flipping through the pages, he commented, "We do not have any lines together until act two scene one."

"I think we should start by reading the lines. It would be best to speak them correctly before trying to act the scene."

Garrett agreed. He looked at the text and read. They switched off until he realized what was coming next. Although this was not his favorite play, he knew it well. His tutors made certain to train him on all classic literature before he left for Eton. Taking a deep breath and wondering what her response would be, he said, ". . . And kiss me, Kate. We will be married o' Sunday."

The words were awkward on his lips. He paused and looked up at Charlotte to see her cheeks filled with a blush.

"No one will expect us to kiss," Charlotte said, holding her hands over her cheeks to cover the embarrassment.

Garrett reached forward and took hold of her hand. He wondered if she was thinking about their kiss. He hoped she was. He wanted to see the red of her face. It gave him a thrill to see how he affected her. "A bit of color in your cheeks looks lovely."

"Please do not say such things."

"Why?" Most women loved compliments. To have her refuse his appraisal was disappointing.

"You are engaged. You should compliment your fiancé."

"About the engagement," Garrett said with frustration, "I do not consider myself engaged. It is a misunderstanding I am trying to correct."

Charlotte took a deep breath, "A misunderstanding? How does one misunderstand a proposal?"

"I did not propose?"

His words had a strange effect on Charlotte. She looked happy but very confused. "I do not understand. Perhaps we should continue with the reading."

Agreeing to her suggestion was better than continuing the confusing discussion of Ruby and the engagement. He looked to the book and said, "There are stage directions in the book. We are expected to kiss." Garrett pointed to the spot in Charlotte's copy.

It wasn't nice of him to tease. She immediately pulled the book close to her face to make certain she saw the words correctly. "You jest, my lord. This is the part of the play where Kate is still angry about everything."

"Not in my copy."

"Then we will follow my copy."

"The directions in my book come from the poet laureate himself. According to Shakespeare, Kate kisses Petruchio." He grinned in the most boyish and mischievous way. For the second time since his farce engagement to Ruby, the burden did not threaten to bury him. His heart was light as a feather and a true smile filled his worried face.

"Let me see what your instructions say." Charlotte reached forward to grab the book out of his hands, but he pulled it away from her reach.

"You did not think I would relinquish this book so easily?" he taunted, holding the book in the air.

"I do not care. My instructions are the true stage directions. Therefore, I trust you will do the gentlemanly part."

"Well, I can be a gentleman but in the end you are the scandalous one who should kiss me."

With an impatient glare, her face going bright red, she continued to speak. "A chaste woman does not initiate a kiss."

The words caught him off guard for a moment. Both Charlotte and Ruby were the ones who initiated kisses with him. They leaned into him. He pushed the thought aside as he remembered how tight Ruby's lips had been during their initial kiss. She was a chaste woman. It was wrong and unfair of him to consider otherwise. Although Charlotte's were not tight, she was the daughter of Duke Ashby, that alone told him she was chaste. Bringing his mind back to the current situation, Garrett looked at the pages of the book. "I do not think Katherine is a chaste character."

"Yes . . . she is!" Charlotte argued taking the book away from him. "What evidence do you have of her lack of virtue?"

Garrett shrugged, "Why would Petruchio expect Kate to kiss him if she were chaste?"

"Are you asking me to portray Kate as a vile woman?"

"I am not the one asking . . ." His words trailed off as he quirked an eyebrow. "Should we make a compromise? Instead of kissing your lips, I could kiss you on your forehead."

"As though you are my father?"

"Well, I do not think I could do it now with such an image in my mind."

"If you want to create instructions, I could slap your face."

"No, it will not do. What if I brush a light kiss across your lips?"

She whispered, "I believe such an action would be unadvisable."

Looking into her eyes, he noticed she did not react as Ruby did when he was near. Ruby would pout and put on a show of begging—a very immature reaction to his presence. Charlotte looked directly into his eyes and met his gaze with a determined stare, showing her maturity. As a side thought, he realized it was best not to verbalize such a thought. Charlotte was far too young to be considered a *mature* lady.

Blue eyes like a clear summer sky—he did not feel mesmerized or lost in her eyes, but he was confused as his heart nearly pounded out of his chest. His voice caught in his throat and he had no idea as to what to say next. He was acting like a nervous schoolboy with his first love. He'd never actually had such thoughts or feelings around Ruby. With Ruby it had been absolute lust toward her beauty.

An unfamiliar feeling of closeness he did not have with anyone else moved through him. Without compulsion, he pulled Charlotte into an embrace and brushed a light kiss across her lips. They were soft and he desired to touch them again.

Ignoring the warning in his head, he pulled her closer and applied more pressure. When she responded by kissing him back, he moved his hand up her back into her hair. The hairband holding her blond locks upon her head fell out as he wrapped his fingers through the silky strands. Another warning rang through his head, telling him to stop, but the thrill of kissing her was better than he'd remembered from the first time, which drove him to further bliss and a complete lack of his surroundings. At that moment there was passion, and he could not hold her close enough to fulfill the desire raging inside him.

Chapter 12

Against her better judgement, Charlotte allowed him to kiss her. Her body was traitorous. Responding was natural and wonderful until she remembered he was engaged. His claim of not being tied down and the engagement being a farce did not matter. If Ruby thought it was real, then Charlotte's actions were those of a wanton woman and there must be some code of womanhood which prevented this type of action.

Engaged! she screamed in her head as she registered the soft, comfortable, smooth . . . She opened her mouth to take a breath and let out a squeak as he deepened the kiss. Filled with a sudden bout of fear, she meant to pull away from his embrace, but strangely was overwhelmed with a rush of confusion mixed with pleasure and light-headedness. Her legs went weak as he pulled her closer and she found her hands holding tighter to him. With these new sensations, she tried to force herself to stop responding, hoping he would notice and pull away, but the intensity only increased as if he were making up for her inattentiveness.

Conflicted, Charlotte responded again as the blissful delight going through her body was too much to ignore. Knowing she needed to end the kiss, but desperate to feel the desire he invoked in her, she had to make the decision to pull away and leave him confused of her feelings or continue to respond and allow herself to be ruined as this intensity could only lead to such an outcome.

With that thought, she decided it was better to end the kiss. But how could she do so, and not leave him in doubt of her feelings?

Charlotte decided she had to swoon.

How does one do so? She was not the type of woman to swoon. She'd never actually seen it happen, but while in London she'd heard of women losing balance and falling down in heated ballrooms. With the decision made, she let her knees collapse. In truth, this did not take much due to the light-headed dizzy rapture she currently enjoyed with his kiss. Keeping her eyes closed, she accepted the possibility of bruises as her knees buckled, her hands released his arms, and her lips tore away from his.

The one part of this she did not expect was for Lord Haughton to be knocked off balance. He fell with her as he tried to compensate for the swoon. Without notice, he was on top of her. Realizing this was not going as planned, it was too late to open her eyes and apologize.

"Charlotte?" Haughton asked as he moved off her body.

Keep calm. Keep your eyes closed. She tried to block his voice to keep from responding by chanting reminders to stay calm and breath normal. Although the kiss frightened her, she'd enjoyed it. The traitorous part of her mind wanted to experience the euphoria of his embrace again. And strangely, she missed the sensation of his touch on her lips.

"Charlotte?" His voice took on a panicked tone as she did not respond. She imagined him looking around for help, and finding they were alone calling out. Instead of making a ludicrous cry for help that wouldn't come, Lord Haughton picked her up from the ground, which she found more romantic.

Worried he would drop her, it took everything she had not to grab hold of him but allow her arms to hang loosely as he carried her to the house. *Why did I choose a location so far from home?* The meadow was a brisk walk from the house, and she'd chosen it for seclusion to be alone with Haughton. With the current predicament, she realized it was a poor choice. *I could not have known he would kiss me!* she argued in her mind, working to forget he carried her in haste.

"What happened to her?" It was either Phillip or Edward speaking. She did not know as their voices were exactly the same.

Lord Haughton tried to respond but was out of breath and had a difficult time speaking. "She collapsed."

There really couldn't be a worse situation for her to be in. If she woke now, would it be too early to be real or should she have woken before now? *Why have I never witnessed a swooning?*

"Phillip, send for Doctor Bell." It must have been Edward. He sounded worried.

This has gone far enough! Although she thought the words, she didn't know how to get out of the situation. *How could I have done this differently? I could have pulled back and slapped him. He deserved to be slapped. He is engaged, to another woman. Although, there does seem to be some confusion on his part. But not on Lady Ruby's!* Suddenly she didn't care about Lord Haughton and his worried tone. He deserved to have a bit of fear thrust in his direction.

Charlotte held out until a smelling salt penetrated her nose. She was lying on a couch, thankfully in the parlor where there was not an audience.

"Lottie," her mother said touching her head and smoothing her messy hair back, "how are you feeling?"

She tried to sit up, but her father and mother pushed her back to the couch. Her father spread a crocheted blanket over her. Guilt increased as she saw her father's concern. Ashby wasn't the most loving man, why did he have to care now? This would be much easier if everyone would leave her alone.

"What happened?" She had to put on an air of confusion so they did not know she was faking her swoon. She looked to the others in the room and noticed Lord Haughton. Unfortunately, Lady Ruby stood clinging to his arm.

"Your face is pale," Phillip said, taking her hand. "How long has Collin been gone? Doctor Bell should be here by now."

"I do not need a doctor. I would prefer to go to my bedchamber."

"Edward, tell a maid to bring cool water in and cloths." Her mother again put a hand on her forehead. "Ashby find out where the doctor is. I do not like the lack of color in her face."

"Mother," Charlotte whispered. "Will you please ask everyone to leave so I can have some privacy?" She was making a terrible fool of Lord Haughton, and the guilt of having him in the room was too much. Seeing him next to Lady Ruby after the passion she'd experienced from his embrace and kiss put an ache in her chest. She held the tears back until it was only her mother with her.

"Do you want to talk about it?" her mother asked in an understanding tone.

Charlotte shook her head in an attempt to hold in the tears. Speaking about feelings and Haughton would only increase the discomfort. Her mother might understand and would give good advice, but did she dare reveal her feelings and the liberties she'd let Haughton take with her? Unable to hold the tears back, she let them fall until the doctor arrived.

Dr. Bell announced a diagnosis of fatigue and prescribed a day in bed, which helped calm her nerves. The day spent in bed was a day of mourning for the relationship she would never have with Lord Haughton, Garrett Calder. Pulling her diary out for the first time in months, she poured her soul into the pages, hoping the revelations to the blank pages would forever seal the feelings she held for Haughton. It might possibly be love, as she'd never experienced the bliss and desire to sigh while around a man. He invoked the best kind of desires in her, and she wanted him to be in love with her.

After reading and rereading her entry in the diary, she cried over the loss of her love and ripped the pages from the book. It would not do for anyone to see the words and know of the designs she'd had for the man. Kissing the pages and holding them to her heart, she vowed to never allow Lord Haughton to kiss her again. Throwing the pages into the fire, she watched as the flames took hold and the pages curled until only ash was left of her thoughts and feelings. With a promise to herself, she stayed in her room until the last possible moment. By the following evening, she was ready to see Lord Haughton again. And she was ready to acknowledge his engagement to Lady Ruby. So much so, she would volunteer to help write the invitations for the wedding.

Chapter 13

While everyone worried over Lady Charlotte, Ruby escaped out to the garden to find Lord Madden. "Joshua," she said as she found him near where she'd first kissed Haughton. Closing her eyes, she decided thinking about her deception with Haughton wouldn't help her in the conversation with Joshua.

Madden pulled her into his arms and held her. "How could you, Ruby? Why did you agree to marry him?"

Wiping at the sudden onslaught of tears his words caused, Ruby tried to explain. She tried to tell him of her father's insistence, but none of it made sense and she only held onto him tighter.

"I will not stand by and watch you marry him."

"I cannot marry him. I will die if I am forced to do so. I love you." She heard her voice. It sounded weak and pathetic. But the words were true.

"Then marry me. Tell me you will be my bride?"

Ruby laughed at the happiness his words brought her. "Yes, yes I will marry you."

Even as she said the words, she knew it would only be possible if they defied her father and left for Gretna Green. Madden bestowed a very ungentlemanly kiss on her lips and moved down her neck. She thought about suggesting they leave now when a loud clearing of a throat sounded through the passion.

"Father?" Ruby said as Madden lowered her to the ground.

"Go to your bedchamber, Ruby."

"No. Lord Madden has requested my hand in marriage, and I have given it. If you continue to disapprove, we will be married in Gretna Green."

Defying her father was the bravest action she'd ever taken. But, did she have the courage to go through with her plan? Taking hold of Madden's hand, she pointed toward the stables. "If we leave now, we will arrive before nightfall."

"Madden, I will pay you handsomely if you leave my daughter alone and never speak to her again."

"You do not have the funds, Father." The whole purpose of Ruby marrying Haughton was to save their family from financial disgrace.

"I have money enough for this."

"Then there is no reason for me to marry Haughton."

"Go to your bedchamber." Her father did not say it as a request this time. Instead, it was a command. Fearing his anger, Ruby ran to her room, tears falling from her eyes. She loved Madden and had every reason to believe he held the same regard for her.

She thought about throwing a tantrum, but it was too much energy. Throwing herself onto the bed, she buried her head in the pillows and screamed. This action alone caused exhaustion. *I do not have the energy to be a brat any longer!* When younger, which really was a strange way of thinking about her age as she was still very young, she would cry and pout until her father relented. Flirting with Haughton took all the energy for pouting and whining. *I cannot believe he accepts my behavior. In truth, there are times I want to hit myself for the fawning I do over him.*

Annoyed neither of her parents had followed her to her room, Ruby sat up and folded her arms in anger. *They cannot force me into a marriage. I am not a child any longer.* Even as she thought the words, she realized how ridiculous they were. She'd been throwing a fit for not getting her way. It was little wonder why her parents continued to think of her as an impressionable child.

Gathering her emotions and burying them under her anger, Ruby ventured down to the parlor where the women congregated to work on embroidery. She vowed, while stitching the words of poetry on a pillowcase, she would find a way to end the situation with Haughton. Madden was her happiness, and no amount of money would change the way she admired him.

Chapter 14

Bonnet in hand, Charlotte set out for a walk into town. While the men were on the morning hunt, the women were to spend time shopping. The town of Ashbourne boasted a milliner, draper, shoemaker, haberdasher, bookstore, and many more shops, which would entertain the women in the party and allow them to find small odds and ends for their projects.

Hoping to work on a new painting, Charlotte found the items she needed to replenish her stock. Remembering the use she and Lord Haughton had put the paints to, she smiled and gathered a few more tubes. *I will have to invite him to paint again.*

As she picked through the options, Ruby's voice drifted over to her and Charlotte stopped her search. *I do not need this much paint, and I cannot invite Lord Haughton to go with me.* Even though he'd kissed her twice, he was still engaged. Although he'd said it was not a real engagement, he hadn't done anything to stop the rumor and Ruby's assumption of marriage. Placing the majority of the paint back, she only took what was needed to replenish her stock.

"Do you enjoy painting?" Lady Lillian asked, fingering the tubes.

This was the first chance she'd had to speak with Lillian, it surprised her the girl would be so bold as to approach. She seemed shy.

"Yes. Did your brother not mention our trip out to the meadow?"

"I saw his face when he returned." Lillian's smile was conspiratorial. She looked to her mother, to make certain they weren't overheard before continuing to speak. "I think he admires you."

Charlotte laughed out of nervousness as she did not know how to respond to the presumption of Lord Haughton's feelings toward her.

Grasping at the visual memory of the paint on Haughton's face, she formulated a response. "It was an entertaining way to end a painting session. I will always count him among one of my dearest of friends."

Lillian gave her a searching look, as though Charlotte's thoughts were written on her face. "He said he behaved very badly and painted you as well."

"Yes." Charlotte tried not to smile too large, as Lillian was far too observant. "Although, I did deserve it."

Lillian stood next to her, rifling through the painting supplies. Charlotte gathered another paintbrush then looked to her new friend. Lillian couldn't be more than eighteen.

"Do you paint, Lady Lillian?"

"Not as well as Garrett, but I do enjoy the practice."

"Would you join me in the meadow tonight or tomorrow? I was thinking about painting the night sky."

"Yes." Lillian bounced on her toes as though she'd like nothing more than to paint with Charlotte. "Perhaps I could bring Garrett?"

"What other pursuits do you enjoy?" Charlotte asked ignoring her question but hoping to become close friends.

Lillian blushed, "Can I confide in you?"

Surprised by the question, Charlotte agreed. Lillian was young, the confession shouldn't be too revealing.

"I want to be honest as to why I want to spend time with you."

Raising her eyebrows, she nodded to let Lillian know she should continue.

"First of all, I would prefer to have you marry my brother. Please do not misunderstand, Ruby is a sweet girl, but she is not Garrett's match. You are. And second, I would like to ask you how to gain Lord Charles's attention? You know him best, as you are his sister."

Charlotte smiled. Ignoring the first part of her comment, she took Lillian's hand and wrapped it through her arm. "Let us walk and discuss my brother."

Purchasing the items, Charlotte smiled at the thought of matching Charles with Lillian. When finished, they exited the shop to walk back to Wentworth Hall as Lord Riley approached. Charlotte looked around, but there wasn't any place to hide, without causing a scene. Resigned to the inevitable conversation, Charlotte stopped along with

Lillian. She nodded, which was polite, but grumbled under her breath while he nodded back.

"Lady Charlotte." He completely ignored all manners as he did not acknowledge Lillian.

Charlotte patted her friend's arm as they continued to walk. She did not acknowledge Riley. "Do not worry at the snub. He is not worth knowing."

"Will you truly ignore me?" Riley asked in his rakish drawl.

"Lord Riley, I thought you were to be on the hunt this morning."

"I was but decided I would prefer to see your beauty instead. Women are preferable to the backside of horses."

Lillian sighed, assuming that his words were romantic. Charlotte groaned. She would have to guide Lillian, especially if they were to be sisters. She planned to be key in Charles and Lillian being married.

"Thank you for the compliment," she said, completely insincere, "but flattery is not the courting I prefer."

"No," Riley said with a glint of anger in his eyes. He dismounted to stand before them. "You prefer to throw yourself at engaged men."

Mouth open, gaping at his insinuation, Charlotte couldn't deny his words. She had allowed Haughton to kiss her. But it was very ungentlemanly of Riley to say such things. Before he could turn away, she slapped him for his rudeness.

"Do not speak to me in such a manner."

Riley's glare ignited with passion. For a moment she was frightened by the glint of anger in his eye, but he wouldn't hurt her, she was certain of it. He might try to ruin her reputation by telling everyone he'd seen the kiss between she and Haughton, but that would be the worst of it. Would anyone believe his words? Would Arundel save her from the rumors? He was her eldest brother and protector.

Grabbing her arm, he squeezed and pulled her closer to him. "Do not get high handed with me, Lottie."

Pulling free of him, she gave a glare worthy of Ashby. "Do not call me Lottie."

She took hold of Lillian's arm and walked as quickly as she could back to Wentworth Hall. She'd need to let Arundel know of Riley's advances. In an effort to move past the unpleasant moment, Charlotte turned to Lillian and attempted to speak with calm. Unfortunately, her voice shook as she said, "We need a plan for you to turn my brother's head."

With a plan in place, Charlotte left Lillian to dress for supper. The men had been out all day with the hunt, but she hoped Charles wouldn't be too exhausted for a bit of flirting. Rushing to his chambers, she knocked.

"Come in," Charles called.

Charlotte pushed the door open and smiled at her brother. "Did you enjoy the hunting party today?"

Quirking his eyebrow as he knew she wasn't there for information on his day, he gave her a quick response. "It was lovely."

"Did you or anyone shoot anything?"

"Birds, it is dinner for tonight. Charlotte, is there a reason you are in my chambers?"

"Yes." She pulled him to the chairs and begged him to sit with her. "Are you enjoying the house party?"

"As much as everyone else is, I am sure."

"What about the ladies. Are there any who have captured your fancy?"

Charles shook his head. "Do not tell me you have a lady you would like me to notice, I care not for the pursuit at this time."

"You are nearly four and twenty. Older than Phillip and Edward were when they chose to marry."

"I would prefer the life of a bachelor, at this time, Lottie."

Charlotte looked down at her hands, disappointed. "There is no way I can convince you otherwise?"

"I believe my brothers have found the perfect women for them, when I am so fortunate, I will make a move."

"But you do not consider any of the women at the party worth your notice?"

"Out with it, Lottie," Charles beckoned tiring of the questions.

"Lady Lillian thinks the world of you. Please give her the opportunity to show you how special she is."

Sighing in exasperation, Charles sat back in his chair, eyeing her with amusement. "When did you become a matchmaker?"

"Oh, this was not my idea. I planned to leave you and Marianne to your own devices, but—" Charlotte allowed her words to trail off, leaving him glaring at her.

Sighing again, Charles responded. "I will speak with Lady Lillian. Only," he held up one finger so she understood him, "if you promise to never try and match me with another woman again."

She kissed him on the cheek. "You know I cannot make such a promise until you are happily wed and settled with a beautiful wife."

Charlotte rushed to leave the room, as Charles asked, "Which one is Lady Lillian?"

Laughing at her brother's complete lack of interest in the women her mother placed in front of him, she said, "She is Lord Cholmondeley's oldest daughter. Beautiful dark brown hair and large inquisitive brown eyes."

He shook his head. "In the future, Lottie, if you are to play matchmaker, please remember I prefer fair hair and blue eyes."

Fearing Lillian did not have much of a chance at turning her brother's head, she rushed to find the girl. Perhaps, Lillian would find she preferred another man.

Chapter 15

Garrett smiled at his sister as she made every effort to flirt with Lord Charles. He was kind but didn't seem to have a desire to match her flirtatious behavior. *Smart man!* Garrett thought as he eyed the pair. If he'd been a little more guarded, he wouldn't be engaged.

"Lord Haughton, are you listening to me?"

Garrett turned to Ruby. "I apologize. My mind was distracted for a moment. What were you speaking of?"

"I wanted to know if you killed the bird we are eating tonight?"

"No. I did not. I spent more time observing the others today." How could her voice cause him to cringe when only days previously he was mesmerized by her every move? He truly did not care for Ruby and could now see the pretentious brat he'd known his whole life. It was strange how her beauty blinded him.

"Why? Are you not here for the hunting?" She batted her eyes at him, as she had always done, but it only proved to frustrate him. He was also annoyed with her constant questions, why could she not let him eat in peace?

"I chose to stand back and allow the higher-ranking men in the party to take the shots."

"Very wise!" Ruby said, giving him a bright smile. "You will do well when you are in Parliament."

Wondering what Parliament had to do with hunting, Garrett nodded in hopes the conversation would end. But it didn't.

"You have a complimentary seat, do you not? As an earl you could claim a spot and participate in the making of laws."

Technically, she was right. But he chose not to claim the seat as he would claim his father's when he became marquess. "It is a bit more complicated and detailed than you perceive it."

"Will you explain it to me?"

"It does not make for entertaining conversation."

Ruby patted his hand and pouted, "I understand, my lord."

Did she understand? He had to guess the answer was no because she continued to discuss his acceptance of a seat in Parliament. "You and the marquess would be a force for good and a great strength, with my father alongside you, if you all had a claimed role. I truly believe it would be wise for you to take a seat at this time."

"Ruby." He hoped to sound patient as he explained his reasonings to her. "My title and my father's title were purchased many years ago by the first Marquess of Cholmondeley. The titles have passed down to my father and I through our lineage. This does not make me qualified to take a seat in Parliament or in the House of Lords, I would prefer to wait until I am ready for the responsibility. My father has agreed to teach me as he is able."

"I do not agree with you, my lord. You were born to this privilege and title and you need to step up."

Taking a deep breath, he smiled at her not wanting to cause a scene in front of the other guests. "We will discuss this later."

As he said the words, he realized he sounded a lot like his father. *When did I turn into him?* It could be worse—he could have turned into one of his uncles. His father was a good man. Turning into him was more a compliment. He shuddered at the thought of becoming one of his uncles: gamblers, drinkers, abusers. Those were just some of the traits he saw in the men. It was shocking to have his family filled with such wicked people when his father was the opposite.

She batted her eyes at him and pouted. He must have missed a comment during his reflections on the family. In her most silky tone she replied, "We will have the rest of our lives to discuss, my love."

The rest of their lives, he repeated to himself. If Charlotte had made the comment, it wouldn't have bothered him. But Ruby did. *Am I simply discontent with what I have?* It was a valid question to ask. Before Ruby assumed they were engaged, he was mesmerized by her. She'd been the one he leaned toward courting. And then he realized he'd finally touched on the crux of the problem. He would prefer to court Ruby, not marry her. He didn't even know the woman. He knew her from childhood, and he hadn't liked her then.

Watching his longtime friends, Arundel and Edward, with their wives made him a bit jealous. There were those among the *ton* who thought it an insult to propriety for people to marry for love, but it worked for the twins. Was it too much to hope for the same?

"My love?"

"Hmmm?" Lost in thoughts he hadn't realized the ladies were leaving the table. Garrett helped her from her chair and sat back in his place for the after-dinner discussion focused solely on the next day's hunt.

His mind wandered to the term of endearment she was now using for him, *my love*, he hadn't realized she'd started calling him such. Did she truly love him? For he now knew what he thought was love at first sight had been merely infatuation. The thought bothered him. He'd known Ruby for many years, how could he have fallen for her beauty? He didn't listen to the conversation around the room, and when it was time to go into the parlor to meet with the ladies, he walked out to the makeshift stables to have a chat with his horse. Sun Dancer would listen and not judge him for his shocking behavior.

Talking to his horse was usually a time for deep reflection. Sun Dancer stood silent while Garrett rubbed behind the horse's ears and spoke about the hunt. "Do you think it is possible to fall in love within a moment?" he asked the horse. Looking into the large deep brown eyes he wondered, not for the first time, if the horse understood everything he was saying.

"I believe it is possible." Looking up from his horse, he turned to see his father approaching. "You looked miserable at dinner tonight. What is the problem?"

Garrett released a deep breath and shared everything with his father. He shared his feelings of Ruby, the misunderstanding about the engagement, the passion he experienced with Charlotte, and the weight pressing down on his shoulders. "My behavior has been less than grand and quite shocking for tender ears. Please do not share this with mother."

"I am trying to understand everything you unloaded on me."

"Would you like me to repeat any of it? Now I have revealed my iniquities, I do not have any shame left."

"No . . . let us begin with the engagement to Lady Ruby. You did not ask for her hand?" Cholmondeley's eyebrows raised in question as he spoke.

With those words, he knew he could trust his father to make everything right. How this would happen, he didn't know. But he was a marquess and had the power to correct indiscretions of his children. Garrett had witnessed this firsthand with his younger brother, who always seemed to be doing something mischievous and shocking. But by the end of the conversation, his father did not have a solution planned, so he had to wait and see what would happen next.

He had too much faith in his father's ability to fix all problems, or so he decided when two days later there was no reprieve. The longer people thought he and Ruby were engaged, the more scandalous the entire situation became.

He had not kissed Ruby since the misunderstanding. He didn't care to be near her, and she occupied her time so thoroughly with wedding plans, she didn't care about his absence. It was a small amount of relief, as he focused on hunting, which also allowed him to stay away from Charlotte. He cared far too much for her and knew the passion they'd shared would draw him back to the shocking behavior he'd displayed the last time they were together.

The evening of the performance for *Taming of the Shrew* arrived far too fast, causing Garrett to groan in frustration. He hadn't picked the book up since his assignation with Charlotte in the meadow.

Thankful his tutors forced Shakespeare down his throat when he was younger, he glanced over the text, trying to memorize as much as he could. *They will not expect perfection.* With this thought, he rushed down to the drawing room, turned theater, and found his place beside Charlotte.

"My lady," he said with a bow in her direction. It seemed an age since he'd last spoken with her.

"I think we should have spent more time practicing," Charlotte said with a nervous bite of her lower lip.

Distracted by her worried stance, and the fear in her eyes, he slowly responded. "Yes, I did consider the same as I came down. If we are equally terrible, perhaps they will find better suited actors for the next performance."

"I pray there will not be a next," Charlotte said with the sincerest expression of angst on her face it made him laugh.

As they were not in the same scene to begin with, he found his place and watched her from a distance. He marveled how each time he spoke with Charlotte, his feelings for her increased. By the time their first scene arrived, Garrett's mind was lost in thoughts of getting out of the engagement and correcting the mess his life had become.

He stumbled over the words for his part, much to the laughter of those in the room. But when the verbal sparring between his and Charlotte's characters started, he paid more attention to her than he did to the audience. He enjoyed the witty way she spoke and wondered if there was a little bit of a shrew inside this woman he adored.

The words affected him far more than he wanted to admit. As she spoke, he internalized each expression as though she were speaking directly to him, which caused him to speak with sincerity to her. The scene he'd spent the day dreading arrived, and with the emotions of the moment, he said the words, "And kiss me Kate . . ." If she responded with her lines, he didn't know. In his despair over the course his life had taken, he considered kissing her in front of everyone in the room.

What would happen if I did? Would anyone care? Of course, they would. It would be the most shocking behavior anyone in the room would claim to have witnessed.

"Haughton?"

Garrett turned as he heard his name to see Arundel prompting him with his lines. Looking back to Charlotte, he apologized to her and the audience and continued the speech. When the performance was finished, he received the award for the *least prepared yet brilliantly performed* actor. Accepting it with a laugh, he pushed his emotions aside and watched with delight as Charlotte and the others received their awards. He wished, if only for a moment, he had thrown out the rules of society and followed through with the kiss.

Garrett thrived in the freedom of riding through the countryside as he joined the morning hunt. Phillip and Edward rode close by, all of them following Ashby's lead. Thinking back on both times he kissed Charlotte and the insane thoughts he'd had the night before while performing, he slowed his horse to fall behind and ponder more about the situation he had put himself in. *I am a rake.* His father still didn't have a solution for his behavior. Waiting for his mother to find out about his actions and threaten to disown him over his dishonorable behavior caused him more than a small amount of stress. He'd been raised to be a gentleman not only in word but in action, and he'd forsaken everything he'd ever been taught on propriety due to the beauty of two women.

Both women invoked feelings in him he never imagined would be a part of his life, which left him very disturbed and unprepared. *It is not a good excuse!* he reminded himself as he inwardly chided his actions. Mesmerized by Ruby's beauty, he'd forgotten his manners. Being near Charlotte threw his emotions over the top and he'd made the poor choices. After kissing her, he knew Charlotte was the one he wanted to spend his life with, ending up with Ruby was a shock to his system. He'd even told Ashby he would offer for his daughter after the fire debacle in the barn.

He had to end the engagement. A man did not simply end an engagement, even when he didn't ask the woman. It would bring ruin on Ruby.

If anyone knew what I did with Charlotte, she would be ruined. Two women faced the censure of the *ton* because he didn't have the self-control to realize which woman he loved in the beginning. The only one who truly had a claim to denounce him was Charlotte. *What was I thinking?* If he could hang his head in shame, he would. His actions with Charlotte had been pleasing but wrong. *It is no wonder she swooned. I treated her like a London whore.*

"Are you unwell?" Edward asked, matching his pace.

"I am well in body, but my mind is overwhelmed." If he could confide in someone, perhaps it would help. Phillip had been through a trying time, and it involved the reputation of two women. With a surge of hope he thought, *perhaps the twins would be able to advise me.*

"We should catch up to the group," Phillip said pointing to where the duke had taken the party.

It was now or he'd never ask the question. His mind was far too muddled to determine if it was a good or bad idea. "If you are agreeable, I would prefer to stay behind. I have no desire to shoot anything today."

The twins looked disappointed but agreed. He knew the sport was a favorite of Ashby's family. "If you would like," Phillip said, dismounting. "Why don't we walk for a bit?"

Garrett followed and held the reins of his horse.

"Is there something particular on your mind?" Edward asked with a ready smile.

"How is Lady Charlotte faring?"

Phillip quirked an eyebrow. "She is well."

"I am happy to hear it." He stumbled on the words, which only made the twins curious.

"Lottie told us of what happened before she collapsed, if that is what you are referring to. What is your excuse?" Edward wagged his eyebrows as if he already knew the answer. There was no reason to keep it back.

The words burst free from his lips as he confessed. "It was supposed to be quick. We were practicing for the performance. One moment built upon another until we were kissing. I behaved terribly. She has every right to call me out before a magistrate. Worse yet, I nearly pulled her into my arms in front of everyone at the performance last night. I think I am losing my mind." Perplexed by his confession, he didn't register the surprise within his audience.

"You kissed our sister?" Phillip asked with a humorless stare.

The blood drained from his face as he answered, "Yes."

"What were you thinking?" Edward asked, taking heed from Phillip's seriousness. All thoughts of laughter forgotten.

Confused, Garrett looked between them. "You did not know?"

"No!" both men shouted.

Ready to cast up his accounts, he turned from his friends. *I have broken their trust.* "I am unwell. I do not think I should finish the activity for the day."

Phillip put a hand on Garrett's arm, causing him to flinch. He expected to be hit. He deserved to be beaten or called out for the inappropriate behavior, taken into the woods and left or shot in a duel. If they wanted to duel him, he would not shoot his gun. He'd allow them to win.

Instead, there was sympathy, especially from Phillip. "I understand more than you know."

Shaking his head, because he was not going to let himself off so easily, he argued. "I do not deserve your sympathy. I know you were also forced into an engagement. I never offered for Ruby. She assumed we were engaged due to a kiss and then one assumption led to another and now wedding invitations are being drafted."

"You are in a mess," Phillip said with a sigh.

Edward's voice trumpeted over the conversation. "What are your intentions toward our sister? You have dishonored her. Ruined her. If anyone else knew about this—"

Putting his hand up, Phillip calmed Edward down with the gesture and a look. "Let us not think the worst. We have known Garrett since Eton. He is a good man."

Shaking his head, he disagreed. "I do not deserve such a compliment."

"Garrett, you need time to think. Do you want us to accompany you back to the house?" Phillip always tried to understand others. He was the most compassionate friend Garrett had.

"Thank you for the offer, but I prefer to go on my own. I have much to consider."

"Consider this while riding back, Haughton," Edward said with a glare worthy of Medusa. "You will restore Lottie's reputation."

Garrett nodded, unable to speak. Ready to turn to stone, yet hoping to avoid the fate, he mounted the horse and put Sun Dancer into a canter. Garrett ran over the same scenarios in his mind each time, hating himself just a little more as he considered his actions.

When he arrived back at Wentworth Hall, he would sit Ruby down and discuss his fears and worries with her, hoping she would understand, and they could mutually break the engagement. With this happy thought as a talisman, he spurred his horse forward until he noticed two people standing off to the right, horses tethered to tree branches.

Even from the distance he recognized Ruby's white hair and Madden's foppish clothing, what he wasn't certain of was the embrace he saw. Knowing it was inappropriate, Garrett dismounted and made his way closer to the couple to see if he was right. This could be the solution he'd been waiting for. Madden could marry Ruby and he would marry Charlotte.

"I cannot continue to pretend to be in love with Haughton. My mother has spent the last week trying to bring sense to my father about this, but the duke is convinced I must marry for money." Ruby's heartbreaking cry didn't evoke sympathy from Garrett.

"I still think we would do best to run away. We could be in Gretna Green by supper. They would not find us in time to prevent the wedding."

Garrett crossed his fingers with hope of this being the final decision. It was not right for him to want Ruby to be ruined, but the intensity of the embrace with Madden was shocking and left Garrett uncomfortable.

He watched them kiss, wondering if he should break into their tête-à-tête with a damning accusation of unfaithfulness, but remembered he'd been in the same situation with Charlotte recently and decided it would be best to speak with Ruby later. Slowly and quietly walking back to his horse, Garrett put his boot in the stirrup to mount.

Happier than he'd been since the phony engagement, Garrett's mind replayed the scene he'd witnessed. He wondered if he and Charlotte had looked as passionate, and nearly laughed out loud when Sun Dancer whinnied. Looking to the ground, Garrett saw a snake slithering into the underbrush. Not yet sitting in the saddle, and not holding tight, Garrett scrambled to pull himself to a safer position as the horse startled, throwing him to the ground.

Angry, as he hadn't been thrown from a horse since he was a child learning to ride, Garrett rolled to his stomach and groaned as he saw Ruby and Madden standing in shocked silence.

Not certain as to what he would say, as he thought he'd have time to gather his thoughts before speaking to her, Garrett let out a slow breath and turned back toward his horse as he heard another loud whinny. His mind didn't process the situation fast enough as he saw the hooves of his horse coming down.

Chapter 16

Ruby screamed as the horse's hooves landed on Lord Haughton's head. Hands over her mouth, she didn't want to watch, but couldn't pull her eyes away from the terrible scene. Madden rushed forward and took hold of the reins, but Ruby stood in stunned shock looking at the battered and broken body of the man she was supposed to marry.

She'd wanted out of the engagement, but never imagined it could happen with an accident as terrible as this. As Madden continued to calm the horse, Ruby ran forward and knelt next to Haughton.

"Garrett?" His name escaped her mouth with a sob. Although she didn't love him, seeing him injured brought a great deal of pain to her heart. Crying as he didn't respond, Ruby wanted to help him but didn't know how.

"Ruby, go back to Wentworth Hall and get help." Madden was by her side. She'd been in shock and hadn't realized he arrived.

"Is he dead?"

"No, Ruby listen to me. We need to bring help out here."

Her mind and vision spun as she stood. Unable to process the entire situation. "I need help mounting my horse."

Leaving Haughton, Madden pulled her in a run back to their waiting mounts. "Hurry, Ruby, bring back help."

She nodded, and when situated on her horse, she rode as fast as she could back to Wentworth Hall. The men were all out hunting, except some of the male servants who accompanied her back to where Haughton lay with Madden by his side.

It wasn't until that evening, when everyone had discussed the entirety of the situation in full that Ruby broke down in tears. She didn't correct Lady Violet and the other prying women when they assured her Haughton would heal and they would be married. This was not her reason for tears.

She was ashamed of her actions. If she and Madden hadn't been in the woods in a secret rendezvous, Haughton wouldn't have stopped. He'd be safe. They'd have supper, play cards, or listen to poetry readings, dance deep into the night and get up in the morning to do it all over again.

Claiming a headache, she slowly walked up to her chambers. Running away to Gretna Green would have to wait for another day.

Chapter 17

There wasn't much Charlotte could do to help Lord Haughton, so she continued to help Ruby with the invitations. As each card was finished, she wanted to cry along with Ruby, as did every other lady in the house.

Lillian and her younger sister hadn't been seen in the common rooms since Lord Haughton had arrived in terrible condition. Madden and Haughton's valet carried him to his bedchamber and sent a servant to find the doctor, who happened to be on the hunt with Ashby and his guests.

"Do not worry, my dear," Ruby's mother said as she piled another round of sweets on her plate. Charlotte watched the woman as she was now on her third plate of cakes and biscuits yet remained thin as ever. "The doctor will set him to right. He will be back on the hunt with everyone else by tomorrow."

Taking a deep breath to calm her nerves, Charlotte tried not to resent the ludicrous comments. Lord Haughton was seriously injured. The servants were tending him, but Doctor Bell wasn't promising Haughton's parents anything in regard to a recovery.

Over the following days, the house party took on a somber tone as Lord Haughton did not wake. Charlotte's mood went from bad to worse as she listened to Ruby for the fifth dinner in a row lament her future as an old maid.

"I will lose him," Ruby cried into her soup. "He will die, and I will be a widow."

Charlotte muttered under her breath, "You cannot be a widow if you were not married."

"I am certain Lord Haughton will wake," Lady Violet said patting her arm.

"No, he will not. It has been five days. You all know what Doctor Bell said. He said the longer Garrett is unconscious the more likely he will stay that way." Pouting in the way she used to when speaking to Haughton, Ruby looked at Charles, Lord Riley, and Lord Madden. It looked as though she were hoping to earn affection from one of them.

Perhaps, Charlotte thought, Lord Madden or Lord Riley would fall in love with Ruby. *Or I can convince Charles to . . . no. I love my brother too much to stick him with Ruby. But he did say he is attracted to fair hair.* In a desperate moment she wondered, *what color are Ruby's eyes?* When the candlelight hit them, Charlotte's hopes dashed, Ruby's eyes were green not blue. She suddenly wondered if Charles only gave her the description due to no woman at the party fulfilling the requirements. She looked to each fair-haired lady to find they either had green, brown, or hazel eyes. *He is impossible!* Making mental note to confront her brother, she went back to focusing on her dinner.

Charlotte watched Ruby over the following days to see if her assumption of searching for a replacement was correct. Lord Madden paid particular attention to Ruby. Riley spent time leering at Charlotte. Charles was kind but did not put forth an effort of flirtation toward Ruby. He seemed to care little for the women in the party until Lady Lillian emerged from her room. She looked downtrodden, and it made Charlotte proud to see her brother step forward and lend comfort. He might not marry Lillian, he would probably remain a bachelor for some time, but he was a good man to have around in a crisis.

The morning marking the first week of Lord Haughton's accident, Lord Cholmondeley experienced a breakdown. In his anger, he rushed out to the stables and vowed to rid his family of Sun Dancer. Charlotte witnessed the fit as she readied for morning exercise with Magenta.

Cholmondeley carried a rifle ready to euthanize the animal. As he lead the horse away from the others, Charlotte worried he'd follow through and kill the horse. Following him, Charlotte cried out. "My lord, Haughton would not agree with your decision."

"He will not ever know," Cholmondeley cried out.

She was thankful her father and Phillip entered the makeshift stables before Cholmondeley raised his rifle. They managed to talk him out of the action. When he was under control again, Charlotte helped by guiding Sun Dancer back to his place.

"Killing the horse will not heal Haughton," Ashby said. Charlotte wondered at her father's softness. It wasn't normal for him to be so compassionate. Taking Cholmondeley's rifle from him, Ashby led the mourning man back to the house while her brother stayed to help her with the horse.

"Is Lord Haughton . . . ?" She couldn't finish the sentence.

"He lives." Phillip blew a frustrated breath out as they backed the horse into the stall. "I do not know how much longer though."

Shaken by the scene she'd witnessed and her brother's words, Charlotte chose to skip her ride and found her way back to the house. Unsurprised to find Collin in the front hallway as she entered, she returned his nod of acknowledgement, as it seemed rude to ignore even a servant. She was to the parlor when his voice echoed in the nearly empty space.

"You mourn for Lord Haughton?"

It surprised her. Collin was turning out to be a very forward servant. She thought about ignoring him but decided to respond. "Lord Haughton is the best of men, so yes, I do feel his absence."

"He is not worth your notice, my lady."

"On the contrary, Collin, it is you who are not worth the notice. Do not speak to me again."

The words escaped her mouth before she could stop them. As she walked away, she experienced a pang of guilt for the hurt on his face. He'd always been kind. But she didn't know what it was about Lord Haughton that Collin disliked so much. His words were hurtful, and she found the need to defend Haughton.

Turning from the parlor, she made her way to the library to avoid company as she wanted to mourn the loss of Lord Haughton. If his father had given up, it made sense for everyone else to do so as well.

As part of a diversion from the sadness pervading the house, a musical was arranged. Charlotte refused to perform. Charlotte paid little attention to her clothing as Haughton was not to be there to admire her and let her maid choose the dress and her hairstyle. Charlotte walked down to the music room out of respect for her mother. She preferred to stay in her chambers locked away in silence while thinking of Haughton. Her heart couldn't handle another night of company and forced joy, but her mother would expect her to attend and that duty kept her feet moving forward in a slow dreaded pace.

As she came to the bottom of the stairs, she noticed Collin standing straight backed against the wall. The other footmen stared forward as their position required, but Collin looked at her. It was unnerving as she didn't care for his attentions. Avoiding the chill his continued gaze left with her, she found a seat between her brothers.

Her mother convinced Phillip to play. Everyone loved hearing him on the piano. The song made her feel hope, which was better than the depression she'd drowned herself in over the previous days. The coldness from Collin's stare left with the sound coming from the piano. The music her brother created brought beauty back to her mind, if only for a moment. She knew Phillip blamed himself for Haughton's accident, which was a ridiculous conclusion to draw since he hadn't been present when it happened. But he'd sent Haughton on ahead by himself. Both Phillip and Edward believed if they'd been there, they could have stopped the accident.

With thoughts of the accident, her eyes wandered over to Lord and Lady Cholmondeley and their two girls, they looked exhausted and distraught. It put a smile on her face to see Charles sitting next to Lillian. Either he was attracted to her, or he was a friend working to comfort her. It was surprising to see the marquess at the evening event. He'd spent more time in vigil at Lord Haughton's side than anyone else. Their relationship was much different than Ashby's was with his heir. The marquess seemed to love his son. She wondered if her father would have paid vigil at Phillip's sick bed.

The thought of her father took her eyes in his direction. He'd been different during this house party. Perhaps it was the lack of Norland in attendance, but she hadn't heard of any outrageous gambling. Phillip would be happy as the bets usually included him. Ashby sat quietly in the audience, at her mother's insistence she was certain, as Ashby did not enjoy music. The only reason he'd agreed to the house party this year was for hunting.

As she continued to look around the room, she noticed Lord Riley and his smug countenance. He sat staring at her as though he could see through her clothing. It was more than unnerving and far too scandalous. To have two men with designs toward her was far too distressing. Collin had no hope, if that was his intention. Ashby would throw him out of his employment without a reference if Collin tried to ask for her hand. Riley was the one she feared, as her father invited him for this purpose.

"My lord." Nate, interrupted Phillip's piano solo.

"Has something happened?" Lord Cholmondeley stood ready to rush from the room.

"Lord Haughton is waking."

Charlotte looked to Phillip and numbly followed as Lord Haughton's family and her brothers rushed from the room. Lady Ruby ran ahead of them all, vowing to be the first person Haughton saw when he woke. Charlotte knew she should wait until he was well and able to leave his chambers, but the desire to see him drew her toward the sick room.

Forced to stand in the doorway, Charlotte watched with anticipation as Lady Cholmondeley asked her son to wake.

Chapter 18

"Garrett, you need to wake up."

He wanted the noise to stop. Tired and in pain, he wanted to stay asleep as he hadn't been in pain until consciousness came over him. But his mother would not stop saying his name. He could hear Ruby's chatter, although he had no idea what she was talking about. Then came the smelling salts. The horrific stench permeated his brain and made his eyes fly open.

"Garrett!" His mother's exasperated voice filled the air around him. "Doctor, he is fully awake."

He blinked. There had to be some sort of a mistake. His mother said he was awake, but it didn't seem possible.

"Lord Haughton, do not try to move."

His body hurt too much for him to want to move.

"Why is he not responding?" Ruby's question made him angry. Remembering he was upset with her, but not finding the details in his immediate memory, he decided not to worry at the moment.

Closing his eyes, he hoped the next time he opened them it would be different. His head hurt. He opened his eyes as his mother again said his name. Everything was the same as before. Speaking for the first time since he woke, he asked, "Will you light a candle?"

His mother took his hand and questioned, "What do you mean?"

"I cannot see anything. Will you turn on a lamp?"

"Doctor? The lamp is lit." His mother sounded frightened, which proved to increase his fear.

"Lord Haughton, can you see your mother?"

Garrett wondered how anyone could expect him to see anything in the dark. He blinked and hoped his eyes would clear. "I cannot see anything. Will you please move the lamp closer?"

Ruby's voice interrupted the doctor's words. "What does he mean? What is he saying?"

"Ruby, now is not the time for hysterics." He'd never heard his father speak with such passion and rudeness to a lady. "Please stay quiet or leave."

"Father?" Garrett panicked. Ignoring the pain in his head and the rest of his body, he tried to pull up from the bed. "What is happening?" His voice cracked as he asked, giving away his fear and worry. Taking deep breaths so he had something to focus on other than the darkness, he waited for an answer.

An answer didn't come. Garrett's confusion increased as he didn't understand what was happening around him. The room erupted in Ruby's hysterical crying, his mother and father yelling at the doctor, and a confusing amount of noise. The deep breathing he practiced only moments before, turned into panic. Suddenly he could no longer take in air. He was suffocating and everyone was too busy arguing to notice.

Unable to sit up due to his injuries, Garrett rolled to the side, hoping air would be easier to find but only managed to cause more pain in his body. Crying out, he caught the attention of everyone in the room.

Time didn't make sense to him as he'd go from sleeping in emptiness to waking in the dark. Since the accident he didn't dream as his mind stopped conjuring images. It was strange, people he'd known his entire life sounded like strangers to him. Deciphering voices, tones, and inflections was an art of which he did not have the skill set. It no longer mattered to him to have his eyes open. As he woke, he lay on the bed, unmoving, listening to the strange world he now inhabited.

The darkness had never frightened him before, but he was now irrationally scared. If he moved, he was worried he'd fall off the bed as he had no idea where the mattress ended. He didn't remember how far it was to the floor, and he'd never paid enough attention to the room to know where things were without sight.

After weeks of lying in bed, it became a routine for him to be there and to be taken care of. He had no plans of making a change. He just didn't know how Ashby would take to a permanent house guest. His parents would have to hire someone to carry him from the house if he were to be moved. Even though the bed was normal, the dark wasn't.

"Mother? Help me?"

Every time he called for her, she rushed to his side. Taking his hand in a comforting way as she tried to calm his fears. "There is no need to fear."

"I need light. Please open the drapes." His breath caught in his throat as the fear froze his body. He hated going through this same dialogue every time he woke yet moving past it would require a strength he didn't have. He knew his injuries were still very real as his leg was in a splint and elevated. The presence of the splint made his entire body feel as though he were trapped and bound with cords. Gasping for air, he clutched his mother's arm, trying to find light.

"Help me!" he croaked.

His mother pulled him into her arms and held him. "Breathe! William, get Doctor Bell."

Living in a never-ending nightmare of darkness was suffocating, but his mother's soft voice helped him calm down to where he could draw air into his lungs.

"Garrett, you are awake?"

He stopped fighting his mother as he heard Ruby's voice. She had not visited him since he woke. "Ruby?" he croaked.

"Garrett, I wanted to speak with you."

"Right now is not the time, Ruby," his mother said as he clung to her. It was like his very existence depended on her holding him.

He stayed quiet wondering if she were there to end their engagement. No one would blame her. He'd heard the whispering outside his bedchamber. Words like, too young to be bogged down by an invalid were fresh in his mind. Although he'd never proposed, the thought of someone loving him enough to stay with him gave a small amount of comfort. Would Ruby give him what he needed? He doubted it. But would Charlotte want him in this condition?

He tried to remember the mesmerizing glow in Ruby's eyes, but the memory was weak. In truth he couldn't remember if they were green or blue. With the confusion he called out, "Ruby, do not look at me. I do not want you to see me in this condition."

"Garrett, there was an accident," Ruby spoke as one would while speaking to someone slow. "You are blind."

As though hearing the words spoken out loud made the dark worse, Garrett shook his head in disbelief. "Do not lie to me. I am not the one who wanted to get married. Just say the words and I will release you. You do not have to make up stories."

His sisters had spoken about Ruby and Lord Madden while they thought he was sleeping. He had a vague memory of finding Ruby and Madden in a secret assignation and wondered if she would ask to be released for that purpose alone.

"Ruby is telling you the truth." His mother's voice cracked. It took every bit of her strength to speak the words. "We are here for you, dear."

Accepting blindness wasn't part of his plan. "My eyes will clear up. They are just a bit foggy."

An understatement to be sure, but if he accepted the idea of being blind, it meant there was no way out of the confinement he was trapped in. Also, he truly did not believe he would stay blind. *Is she staring at me? Are they all looking at me?* "Get out!"

"What?" Ruby sounded hurt, but he'd already told her he didn't want her looking at him.

"Leave." Yelling at everyone in the room, he sounded like a spoiled child. "I do not want you in here looking at me."

"Garrett, calm down," his father called out in frustration.

"I do not need your pity."

Clearing his throat, his father said in a deep brash voice, "I do not pity you, boy. I expect you to get out of this bed and do your duty as my heir."

Garrett crumbled at his father's words. *How can I take my place in Parliament? How can I be the Marquess of Cholmondeley? I cannot! Not like this.* He sobbed into his mother's arms. Accepting the darkness was not an option. This was a moment of déjà vu. He'd sobbed into his mother's arms more than once since waking in the dark.

"Doctor, what is wrong with him? Is he insane?" Ruby's voice broke through his self-pitying thoughts.

"Insane?" he whispered in his mother's shoulder. *No, I am not insane!* Instead of speaking, he waited for the answer. If the man responded in the positive, he'd make certain his parents found a more competent doctor.

The doctor sighed, "No, Lady Ruby, he is not insane. He needs to come to terms with his new reality."

Hearing his thoughts confirmed, Garrett allowed a moment of peace to come over him as the doctor confirmed insanity was not an issue. He needed to hear more. Needed to know he would heal and be all right.

"I do not understand. He should be fine." Ruby's voice was pouty. He recognized the sound even without sight.

"What do you expect to see when you open your eyes every morning?" Garrett listened to the doctor hoping there would be some sort of relief for the distress he was experiencing.

"I see my maid, and if she is not there, I ring for her. My bed here at Wentworth Hall faces the windows, so I love it when my maid opens the drapes and I am able to see out across the front gardens."

Garrett wanted to tell her to stop speaking, as her words only brought him pain. He clutched his mother tighter, wishing everyone would leave.

"I expect to see light," Charlotte's voice raised over Ruby's making the constant self-pity stop.

"Lady Charlotte is correct," Doctor Bell said.

What is she doing here? He didn't know how he felt about Charlotte being in his room. He didn't want Ruby there, but Charlotte! Just her name in his thoughts brought peace. If she were to stay with him, he might be able to break through the darkness and regain his sight.

"Imagine waking every morning and instead of light, all you see is dark. You do not see shapes. Waving a hand in front of your face does not bring motion to your senses. Rubbing your eyes does not bring clarity—"

The doctor continued to speak, but Garrett's mind was focused on Charlotte. She was here. She was not repulsed by his condition as there was no requirement for her attentions. Those thoughts brought clarity and light to his mind. He could not see, a fact still troubling him, but was her presence a beacon of her love for him?

"— no, he is not insane. He is frightened," Doctor Bell finished.

"But you can heal his eyes?" Ruby asked hopefully.

Her words dashed the wonderful feeling of hope he'd built with Charlotte's presence. *I am still engaged to Ruby.*

"No, Lady Ruby, I cannot heal his eyes. Lord Haughton will remain blind."

These were words he'd been dreading yet waiting to hear. Words no one had been willing to speak around him for days. His anguish at waking up in darkness buried him in hopelessness. Garrett let go of his mother and lay back on the pillows. With the last simple statement, his future was sealed. *I will never see again.*

He didn't expect Ruby to throw herself on the end of his bed, but she did. Thankfully it was a larger bed and his leg was not further injured. Closing his eyes, he listened to Ruby's sobs mixed with other females in the room. *Is one of them Charlotte?* Something told him she wasn't crying. Charlotte possessed a strength of character Ruby didn't have. Not many women could be as graceful and kind as Charlotte.

Chapter 19

Being dragged from Lord Haughton's side while she cried over his loss of sight was embarrassing, but her hope was to put the rumors of her relationship with Madden to rest. She needed everyone, especially her father, to believe she was in love with Haughton and distressed. The latter wasn't difficult to do, as she was horrified with having witnessed the accident. It was the emotion of love that proved to be a challenge.

"Ruby, since you are engaged to Lord Haughton, you need to perform your duties." Her mother and father sat her down in their sitting room to discuss her role.

"Mother, what if he does not regain his eyesight?"

"I have no doubt it is temporary." Her mother's words did not lend comfort.

"I cannot marry an invalid. I am too young." She did not want to sound like she was whining, but her concerns were more than valid.

"Showing anything but sympathy right now will get our family thrown out of Wentworth Hall," her father said looking around his newspaper. "We cannot appear to be anything but worried about Lord Haughton's condition."

"Why would it hurt to leave right now?" Ruby asked pouting and stomping her foot in frustration. This tactic worked on her parents when she was younger, why wouldn't it work now?

"Start behaving as a lady!" her father demanded. "We do not have the funds to support ourselves for an entire year."

Ruby looked down at her hands. *The financial blunder must be worse than I thought.* "I am concerned about him, father."

"Then play your part well."

"What part?" Ruby didn't understand her father. "You told me to get a proposal from him, so I did. I hardly even know him."

"You are engaged to an injured man. You will stay by his side as is proper and you will help him through the healing process." Her father's words were never questioned, but she did not love Garrett.

"Father, with Lord Haughton's injuries no one would place blame if I broke the engagement. I should not have to care for a husband in such a condition."

"Who do you suppose you will marry, if not Haughton?"

"Lord Madden?" she squeaked.

"Madden is a younger son of a duke. He will not inherit a title or a place in Parliament. He has no influence and will not be able to help our financial situation."

Ruby hung her head in frustration and sadness. Ruby didn't want the tears pooling in her eyes to fall in front of her father. She turned away from him to hide her shame.

"We each must do our part, Ruby."

Her parents had given her this information before arriving at Wentworth Hall. She'd agreed to marry the highest-ranking bachelor to help the family and she couldn't back down now. Gaining control of her emotions, she nodded to her father and left to commiserate in her fear and heartache.

Ruby walked through the garden trying to find a way to go back into Lord Haughton's chambers. She needed to spend time with him and help him through the difficulty of healing. But each time she stopped crying it only took a quick thought of what she was giving up with Lord Madden before she'd start sobbing again.

"You need a handkerchief."

Ruby's tear-stained face turned toward the man she loved. "Lord Madden, I thank you for offering."

Taking the handkerchief, she wiped at the tears and made certain there weren't any unwanted leaks from her nose. "Thank you." She tried to hand it back to him, but he held out his hand to let her know she could keep it.

"What brings you to the garden today?"

"I was looking for a break from the sadness in the house and happened upon you out here." Madden's tone was sincere, which caused her to tear up again. "I have no doubt Lord Haughton will heal."

In a moment of weakness and anger with her father, Ruby lashed out. "I do not want him to heal. I want to be free of him. And if he does heal, do you think he will keep our jaunt in the woods a secret?"

"Ruby, you want him to heal. I know you do. Your reaction when we saw him injured was enough to let me know you have feelings for him."

Bravery born of her outburst, she continued, "If he does not heal, we can escape together. This is my father's doing."

She turned from the man she loved in shame. *Why would he want to marry me now? I am making a ninny out of myself. A woman should not declare her feelings so openly.*

"I know you do not love him, Ruby. But wishing him unwell is not like the beautiful person I have come to love."

Ruby shook her head. "I am sorry. I do not wish him injury. I love you and want to be with you."

"I am wealthy, Ruby. Please speak with your father and tell him I can provide for you as well as Haughton can. I know I will not inherit my father's title, but I will have a house." She looked up to gauge his sincerity and found only admiration and love. "Ruby, if you will have me, I will make a generous husband."

This was his second proposal in a month. She'd accepted his request the other night, he was now requesting again, making her believe he'd die without her.

Madden leaned forward and pulled her into his embrace. "Ruby, I have cared for you since we met in London last year. If you only desire my friendship, please tell me now, but you have to end this farce with Haughton."

Ruby sobbed on his shoulder until she no longer had tears. "I do not know how we will accomplish this, but I will be your wife."

Chapter 20

The weather matched Charlotte's mood, dreary. Lord Haughton and Lady Ruby were still on course for marriage. This was a development she did not think was possible, given Ruby's flirtation with Lord Madden. But what did Haughton know of it? He was too busy learning how to live without eyesight.

She wanted to see him. The kisses they'd shared stayed with her, and in the quiet moments of the night she'd reflect on the emotions he inspired in her. It had to be love. Wishing she could find a moment to herself, she made her way to the library. It was strange how she could be so lonely with a house filled with people. With the library door partially opened, Charlotte moved to enter when her father's voice rang out over the silence of the hallway.

"We will have to call off the bet, Dudley. Cholmondeley is too distraught to continue, and I believe my son would have won for me anyway."

"What makes you think Arundel would win?" Dudley asked with a laugh.

Charlotte thought about leaving but decided it would be best if she knew what the bet was. Poor Phillip would never get away from the man's scheming.

"Arundel is already married. He and his wife will have a child long before Haughton and Ruby do."

Charlotte's mouth dropped open. *He is gambling based on grandchildren.*

"If you recall, Ashby, the bet is not based on who produces a grandchild first, it is who produces an heir. My daughter and her intended have more than enough time."

"I doubt Haughton will be able to produce a child in his condition."

"The doctor confirmed there was not damage to Haughton's—"

Charlotte's eyes went wide as she anticipated the next words. She turned away from the library so she wouldn't be privy to her father's lack of propriety. *Do Phillip and Emma know about this bet?* she wondered as she walked to her bedchamber. Since his marriage, he and Emma spent the majority of their time at Arundel Keep in the south of England. They were only at the house party due to their mother's insistence that all of her children attend. But both Phillip and Edward kept themselves and their wives away from Ashby as much as possible.

The bet bothered her even more because of the inclusion of Cholmondeley. She thought he loved his son. A man who loved his child wouldn't enter into a gamble on something so personal. Was this engagement truly a farce?

With the need for information, Charlotte changed paths and moved toward the sick room. She needed to speak to Haughton. Needed to know if he were aware of the gamble. She would not go in alone, as it would not be proper, but she would get the information no matter his current condition.

When she arrived, the door to his chamber was open. Lacking the desire to overhear another conversation, she knocked and waited for approval to enter. It put a smile on her inquisitive face to see Phillip and Edward doing their best to entertain Haughton. He gave obligatory smiles as Edward spoke, but it was obvious the last thing on Haughton's mind was laughter.

"Mind if I join you?" Charlotte asked entering the room.

Phillip and Edward stood as she entered. She cringed as Haughton tried to pull himself out of the chair. His leg was not yet fully healed and it looked to cause him pain.

"Please, Lord Haughton, do not stand. No one would fault you for staying seated with the injuries you've incurred." Charlotte rushed to sit next to Edward so the men could retake their seats.

"Edward, I apologize for interrupting your narrative."

"I think the story was overtold," Phillip said standing to leave. "Edward, will you join me in the hall?"

Edward gave a small shake of his head. "My stories are so unappreciated."

She laughed at the smile on his face. She truly did love her brothers. They were the best of men.

Edward pulled on Phillip's arm. "We will be across the room, not listening to a word you say, Lottie. But I will warn you, Haughton, my sister's lips are off limits today."

Charlotte's face burned with embarrassment. "Edward!"

"We know about the tête-à-tête you had in the meadow and the stables," Edward said with a wink.

"Will the two of you please mind your own business?" Charlotte glared her brothers into silence. *And to think, I thought they were gentleman!*

"Of course, my lady." Edward and Phillip both gave an exaggerated courtly bow. Her brothers loved to tease and a part of her enjoyed it. But the kissing was a sore subject for her. She feared anyone finding out yet wanted to experience the thrill again. Turning back to Lord Haughton, she noticed he didn't look amused. He couldn't see the silly exaggerated motions of her brothers. He sat waiting for her to speak. The realization of his loss made her sad. The last thing she should do though, was pity him. Pity wouldn't do any good.

"I wanted to speak with you. I miss your friendship." Charlotte thought reminding him of what they once had would be a start. It was a short friendship, yet one equal to a Shakespearean romance in her estimation.

Lord Haughton closed his eyes as though the words were difficult to hear.

"Are you unwell? Do you have a headache?"

"I am as well as anyone can expect." The first words he'd spoken since she'd entered the room were dry and emotionless. Did he not miss her? Did he not want a friendship with her? Surely, she could not ask him about the wager in this current state of distress.

"Now your leg is healing, you should spend time in the garden. It is a little cold and dreary, but the fresh air is nice. We could take you out in the wheelchair." She tried to keep her tone happy and cheerful to brighten his mood, but it didn't seem to work.

"I have no desire to go out to the gardens." Again, his tone was emotionless. She wanted to shake him and bring him back to the person he was before the accident.

"Nature is helpful for recovery."

"Why would I want to go somewhere when I cannot see what it looks like?"

Taking a deep breath so as to not allow the curt and rude words hurt, she paused to consider the next statement. Changing tactics, she asked, "Do you not miss me?" It was not her right to ask. He was engaged to Lady Ruby. Nonetheless, her heart ached to know if he loved her as much as she him. Not caring her brothers were standing a few feet away, she reached forward to touch his hand.

He accepted the gesture and held her hand until one of her brothers cleared his throat, rather loudly.

"I am not supposed to miss you. It is not right."

"I agree, but it does not stop how we feel. Lord Haughton, do you want to continue the engagement? You told me it was not real. Were you truthful?" As she said the words, she realized how childish it sounded. Breaking an engagement was not a simple process. It would require Ruby ending it and there would need to be a valid reason.

Haughton gave a dry, tortured groan. "Charlotte, I owe you an apology. I should never have kissed you."

"Please, do not apologize." She wanted to look away but was unable to do so. He sat broken in spirit in a plush overstuffed chair. She noticed the chairs had been moved, as the last time she was in here they were near the windows.

"I will not ever speak of it again, and nor should you." He pulled himself up from the chair and bowed in her direction. "If you will excuse me, I would like to rest now."

Phillip moved to Haughton's side. His limp was still visible as he walked. Would Lord Haughton now have a limp? They walked slowly across the room. She locked eyes with Edward and exchanged an expression of sadness, then left.

Charlotte spent the rest of her day in the dreary company of others. The house party went on without Lord Haughton in attendance. It'd been this way since the accident. His absence was noted but forgotten as people enjoyed themselves. It made her upset to think life could continue while the man she was convinced to be the only opportunity she had for happiness and love was suffering in the dark. Charlotte looked over to Ruby. She was again leaning on Lord Madden's shoulder, crying.

I will take control of this situation. She does not love Haughton as I do. She plotted while she sipped tea and acted like she cared about the conversation on embroidery.

"Lady Charlotte, might I steal a moment of your time?"

She didn't have to look at the man to know it was Lord Riley. Choosing to show her contempt for the man, she said "No, I am currently occupied."

"No one will miss you in the conversation." He took hold of her elbow and tried to force her out of the chair.

Refusing to go with him, Charlotte made a scene of spilling her tea on Lord Riley. "I do apologize for my clumsiness, my lord."

Riley's glare left her with an uneasy feeling. Something told her she'd pay for her unwillingness.

"Lady Ruby, do you need help with the invitations again?" It was quite possible to expect Ruby was inviting all of England to her wedding. There were more invitations for this wedding than were sent out for both Edward and Phillip's weddings combined. The first part of her plan to end this ridiculous engagement would be to convince Ruby of her indifference toward Haughton.

"Yes, I would appreciate the help."

Charlotte noticed two different stacks of invitations. One larger than the other. She wanted to ask what the difference was but decided to watch and see if there was a distinction.

"What do you think of Lord Madden?" Lady Ruby asked as she finished yet another invitation.

Charlotte didn't start writing. She held her pen mid-air to think of a response. She needed to be careful as they spoke. If she praised

Madden too much, it might cause Ruby to try matchmaking. "He is very amiable."

"I think you are right. He is admirable."

Charlotte went to agree, and then realized Ruby had changed her word. She'd said amiable. "I do not know Madden well. Did you know him before this party?"

"Yes. I met him in London."

"Oh." This was a surprise. Charlotte knew she could work with this information.

"Can you keep a secret?" Ruby asked, eyes sparkling with intrigue. This was not the way Charlotte imagined the conversation going, yet curiosity burned within her and she had to agree.

"Yes, you may confide in me." *Can I keep a secret? Will I keep her confidence? Yes!*

"I am in love with him. It is all very scandalous!" Charlotte noted the excitement and sparkle in Ruby's eyes as she said the words. For a moment she regretted the hope of convincing Ruby to end the engagement. If Ruby were actually in love with Haughton, it would be wrong for Charlotte to put her feelings above another. Perhaps it was true love between Haughton and Ruby after all.

"With Lord Haughton? I would hope you are. You are marrying him."

Ruby blushed. "Can you believe, I am still writing out invitations?" She looked at the card in her hand and put it on the pile closest to Charlotte.

Disappointed with the revelation of her undying love for Haughton, Charlotte found a way to go back to the invitations. "You seem to be inviting a lot of people to the wedding."

"It would appear as such—" Ruby's voice trailed off. She looked down at the invitation she was constructing and finished it only to put it in the other pile. The one closest to her.

"If you have a list, I can address the envelopes." Charlotte pulled both stacks of invitations over. Ruby grabbed one of the stacks in a very unladylike manner knocking a bottle of ink over in the process.

"I apologize if I've overstepped."

Ruby sighed and handed the invitations over. "Please do not tell anyone."

Looking at the parchment in her hand, Charlotte's promise of silence turned to question. Shocked at what she saw, she had to ask, "What are you doing?"

"I am in love with Lord Madden. I am certain of it. He is so kind and attentive. I have been in love with Madden since I met him in London."

Head spinning at the revelation, Charlotte's eyes went wide with the possibilities of successfully ending the engagement between Haughton and Ruby. Surprising even herself, her protective side took over. "Lord Haughton is injured. He is the best of men, even better than Madden." *Why am I defending him? This is what I have hoped for.* "Has Madden imposed upon you?"

"No, he is a perfect gentleman." Ruby looked shocked at the question.

"I think we have misunderstood each other. You are engaged to Lord Haughton, but you are also hoping to marry Lord Madden? This does not make sense and is quite shocking!"

Ruby's face went red. "Madden asked me to marry him."

"Ruby! How could you do this to Lord Haughton?"

Without answering the question, Ruby grabbed both stacks of announcements and rushed from the room while angrily yelling, "When you are engaged to an invalid, you may judge me. Until then, keep to your own affairs."

Charlotte no longer had any guilt for the kisses she's shared with Haughton. Rushing to the meadow for time alone, Charlotte paced in front of a large tree talking to herself.

"How could Ruby be so childish? She is engaged to two men. Planning a wedding to both of them!" She didn't intend to yell out, but as her frustration and anger built, the words escaped her mouth. There were many times she could see her father's temper coming out in her.

"Charlotte? Would you like to discuss your frustrations?" Closing her eyes at her imprudent decision to hold an impromptu conversation with herself, she turned to see Emma, Anne, and Marianne standing behind her.

Losing her composure, Charlotte burst into tears. The loss of her chance at a marriage weighed heavy on her heart, but to lose the man to a woman who had two proposals was suffocating. *She couldn't love both men!* Remembering she'd promised to hold Ruby's betrayal confidential, she decided to sit on the ground and tell them about her broken heart.

She sobbed as she spoke, not certain if they understood her words because it all sounded like gibberish. If she thought talking about her feelings would help relieve the hurt, she was wrong. Her sisters listened, offered advice, and let her cry. When she was finished sobbing, Charlotte lay against Emma's shoulder. The tears didn't stop, she was certain they'd never stop. There were some disappointments in life that caused eternal pain, which brought eternal tears, and this was one of them.

Chapter 21

Time moved dreadfully slow as he lay in bed. Garrett sat up to the sound of a gasp. Was it one of his sisters? His mother? Ruby? *Please not Ruby!* A discussion with Ruby would be too much for him at this time. Her voice grated on his nerves. Conversations with her took too much energy. He would have to find a way to recognize people without having to ask.

"Who is here?"

"Lillian and Hazel," Lillian's voice came through the dark. She took hold of his hand and squeezed it.

"Where is mother?" Since he'd woken without sight, he constantly wanted his mother near him. The comfort of her arms didn't make blindness right, but it gave him peace and safety.

"I will find her. Mother and Father are with the doctor." Hazel's voice. Hazel rushing away. Movement happened too fast for him in this condition.

"Doctor?"

Lillian squeezed his hand. "Yes, a new doctor arrived this morning."

Due to a dry mouth, Garrett reached out to the side table where he knew a glass usually sat.

"Do you need something?" Lillian's voice.

"I would appreciate a drink of water."

Lillian must have watched their parents assist him. She took his hand and guided him to hold the glass. Still unable to perfectly drink due to a lack of perception, he accidently hit his tooth. The momentary pain caused him to drop the glass. Water spilled out on his clothing and bed.

"What happened?" their father shouted.

Voice shaking, Lillian responded. "It is my fault. I should have been more thorough and helped him with the water."

I do not need help. I am an adult. He wanted to say the words out loud, and possibly would have if his father hadn't lost his temper.

"Your brother is blind, Lillian. He cannot see." Cholmondeley never yelled at them. Never raised his voice at his daughters. He doted on them constantly. To hear his father yell at one of them was far too shocking. "If you are unable to assist your brother, you need to let us know."

Lillian burst into tears trying to explain herself, which came out in a blubbering mess. Garrett wanted to take responsibility. Leaning forward, he reached for her hand but was unable to find his sister to give her comfort.

His mother spoke before he could call out. "Girls, please go out to the garden and take some air. Your father and I desire a private word with your brother."

Before they could leave, he called out, "Lillian, it was my fault, not yours. Do not be distressed."

"Go now," his father said in the same angry tone as before. Then softening, he apologized to Lillian.

Eyesight was not necessary to know the stress his parents were under. Yelling at the girls was more than enough for Garrett to realize his father was to his breaking point. "Lillian, Hazel," Garrett called out hoping they were still close enough to hear, "you will both come back to visit me?"

"Yes, of course we will." Both girls hugged him before leaving. He wanted to convey a lot of emotions in the hug, but there was not time. At least his sisters knew he loved them. As the door to his bedchamber closed, someone sat on the edge of his bed. The mattress moved and the smell of cologne told him his father was the one next to him.

"Garrett, I want to talk to you about the new doctor we have brought in for you."

He'd heard the discussion between his parents, Doctor Bell, and Ashby. It was time to get him out of the bed. Out of the bedchamber. In order to do this, they needed to find a specialist who worked with the blind. Doctor Bell suggested a friend, and from what he was now hearing, his parents followed through with hiring the man.

"He teaches the blind." His father's words stopped.

Confused, Garrett asked, "What is he supposed to teach me?"

"How to function in your new state."

Taking a deep breath, Garret tried not to sound juvenile. "Will he be able to teach me how to manage an estate without eyesight?"

"We will take things slowly." His father's tone was hesitant and uncomfortable.

"There is no need to work with this person. I am not blind. My eyes will clear up with rest." *Do I believe this?* He mentally checked his words. They'd come out with so much passion and hope he hadn't expected to say them. Yes, he'd thought many times about how his eyes would heal, but he'd never formed the words.

"It would make your father and I happy if you would try to work with Doctor Moore." His mother's plea fell on stubborn ears.

"Mother, I have no need to learn how to count my steps and function without sight. I will heal." *Why am I fighting them? What purpose is there in arguing? I am blind.* The realization of his situation came back to him. "Send this new doctor away."

"No, I am your father and I expect you to listen and learn."

It was rare for his father to invoke absolute dominance over his children. They'd been raised well and were allowed to make their own decisions.

"I am an adult. I can make my own choices." He still didn't understand why he was arguing. He did need the help.

"You are my heir, and you will let Doctor Moore teach you how to perform daily tasks."

He'd meant to speak to his father about the status of *heir*. His father would need to name his younger brother, James, as the one to inherit. He was now unable to accept a role among the peerage and lord over the estate in Cheshire.

"I have wanted to speak with you about—"

"Not now!" his father interrupted.

"We have to have this discussion at some point." If they wanted him to be realistic about his sightless situation, they would have to accept the reality of his father needing a reliable heir. One who could help with the responsibilities.

"Work with the doctor, then I will listen to you." His parents must have left, because he heard the door open then close. He sat tense, wondering if the doctor was in the room already or if he was alone. It'd been a long time since he'd been alone. His curiosity was answered within minutes with a knock on his door.

"Come in."

Doctor Moore started teaching him early in the morning and did not give up until long after the supper hour. For the first time since he'd fallen from his horse, Garrett was exhausted and could sleep soundly. It was wonderful.

Walking across a room while counting steps wasn't as bad as he originally made it out to be in his mind. It helped him get from one side of the room to the other without tripping over things. He learned to eat with a knife and fork again, but this time without looking at his plate. Moreover, one day, with a great deal of work, he could still enjoy reading once he learned how to use braille.

For the first time since the accident, Garrett was actually happy he survived. The full memory of what happened was vague, he'd never fallen from a horse. As an expert rider and a person who cared deeply for the animal, it was a confusing notion to think the horse would suddenly throw him. Ruby and Madden claimed to have found him lying on the ground after the accident. But there was something to that as well, as he was certain he'd seen them in a private tête-à-tête.

The more he learned with the doctor, the more confidence it gave him to realize he would be able to have a full life, but a nagging doubt told him he wouldn't be able to be his father's heir. His goal each morning was to have the discussion with Cholmondeley, yet each day his father avoided him when the topic arose.

Determined to have the conversation, he grabbed the cane the doctor gave him, and left his room, hoping his memory of Wentworth Hall was enough to get him to the parlor. It was morning, and his parents would be there with the other house guests. Each step became a calculation in his mind. Although he'd never enjoyed mathematics, he pictured walking as a problem to solve.

Once he was to the bottom of the stairs, an overwhelming desire to see Sun Dancer crossed his mind. He redirected and headed out to the temporary barn. He hadn't seen his horse for far too long. Each step was an effort and brought temporary fear until he moved to the next without tripping or walking into something. Noises he'd never noticed when sighted brought new meaning to life. His boots against the ground made a shuffling sound, he vowed to walk without a shuffle once his leg was fully functioning again. Birds and other creatures made noises indicating their presence in the world.

Was he going the right way? Would he make it to the horses? Far too many times he thought about turning back and going up to the safety of his bedchamber, but before long he was lost and did not know how to make it back to his room.

Confidence down, now he knew his memory of Wentworth Hall wasn't great, he decided to find a bench to sit on. The purpose of the cane was to help navigate around items, but he didn't know a tree from a bush or a water fountain from a bench without using his hand.

Blocking the angst as he walked hand out in front trying to touch or find a bench, he searched for anything to tell him where he was. *When I get back to my bedchamber, I will never leave it again! Am I a coward? Yes!* At first the answer to the question bothered him, but after thinking about trying to find his way back to the house, he decided being a coward was just fine. Admitting he was frightened wouldn't be difficult. His search produced a bench, so he sat and decided he wouldn't move until someone with sight was able to guide him to his bed.

Garrett had only to wait a few minutes before he heard his father calling his name. Thankful for the rescue, he didn't mind his father's reprimand for frightening everyone. As he was deposited back in his bedchamber, he wished he'd been more daring.

"Father, can we discuss my title?"

"Not now."

It was a way to avoid the situation. "When will be the right time?"

"After you start eating in the dining room again."

"You are expecting a miracle. I do not want to eat in front of people." *Why do they not understand?* Sitting in a room while people watched the blind man eat was not on his list of items to do. He'd prefer to eat by himself.

"It sounds as though we are at an impasse."

Garrett closed his eyes and sighed. He noted the pain as he tried to move his eyes in a circle. Why he tried to do so, he didn't know. "How can I help you understand? I am not comfortable eating with everyone."

"What will you do once you are married?"

"Ruby already considers me an invalid. She knows what she is getting in a husband." Finding his way to a chair, he continued, "I am surprised she hasn't ended the engagement. I have wondered why she continues to plan. She is capable of finding another husband." Then remembering a conversation he'd had with his father about the situation, he asked, "Have you not yet found a way to relieve me of my mistake?"

He thought his father might have left during his rant as there was not an immediate answer. *Blindness was very annoying!* Sighing as he turned to where he was certain his bed sat, he walked to it when his father finally responded. "Your mother and I will speak with Dudley about the engagement. We do not believe it is wise to continue planning at the moment. Perhaps when you are well."

"I will never be well again. And you know I had no intention of proposing to Ruby. She only assumed we were engaged." The harsh tone he used was new since the accident. Garrett respected his parents, but the anger he had in him due to the blindness didn't seem to ever dissipate.

"You cannot give up hope, and it has been far too long to claim the engagement was a misunderstanding."

"What would you have me hope for? A life where I can be the Marquess of Cholmondeley while blind? I would be the laughing-stock of the *ton*. Watch me take a seat in Parliament and tip my drink over while everyone bursts into laughter." He chose not to touch on the comments about the engagement. Truthfully it had been too late when Ruby announced the debacle to everyone. He would have continued to speak but his father took hold of his hands.

"This is the reason we have hired the doctor. He is to teach you so you can do these things."

"It is pointless!"

His father took hold of his chin, as though he expected Garrett to look into his eyes. The joke was on Cholmondeley as Garrett could not see him. "If King George III could run a country without sight and hearing, then my son can be in Parliament."

Garrett laughed, "King George III?" It was a ridiculous comparison. "The king had servants and advisors."

"As will you!"

Shaking his head, he tried to formulate an argument but couldn't find the words to express his concern, at least words he hadn't already tried. "I would like to be alone."

He hoped his father truly left as he didn't want any company. Brooding over the situation wouldn't do him any good, but it was what he planned to do.

Chapter 22

"What brings you out to the patio tonight?" Charlotte cringed as she looked toward the stars. Recognizing the voice of their ever-annoying footman, Collin, brought chills on this very warm evening.

"I should think you are the one overstepping," she spoke without looking at him. The desire to view the stars was a much happier thought than his face. She still hadn't forgiven him for the censure he'd shared over her attachment to Lord Haughton.

"You are still angry with me?" Collin asked.

Again, looking away from him, she gave an audible sigh before responding with one word only. She didn't owe him an explanation, he was the help. "Yes."

"What can I do to receive forgiveness?"

Wanting him to leave her alone, Charlotte rolled her eyes and turned from the beautiful night sky. If she could send him on his way, she could get back to the search for constellations. "There is no need to ask my forgiveness. Now please, leave me in peace."

Her words were brash and cut his confidence down. Surprisingly, this didn't bother her. He had changed since the house party started. Collin was, at one time, someone she would consider a friend. Now, with his condemnation of Lord Haughton, she wanted nothing to do with him.

"You still care for him? After all of my warnings, you still hope for a future with that rake?"

"Lord Haughton is not a rake." It didn't take any thought to defend the man she knew she was in love with. She thought of him when she was awake, dreamt of kissing him when sleeping, and hoped above all else he would break free of Ruby and ask for her hand in marriage.

"He is engaged to Lady Ruby. Throwing yourself at him does not paint a picture of virtue."

Charlotte closed her eyes in an attempt to find peace. When she opened them to address his last statement, she started by slapping his face. "I warn you, Collin, to never speak of my virtue again. It is none of your concern."

Collin grabbed her wrist and pulled her toward him. "I plan to marry you, and I will not take a wanton as my wife."

Breaking free of his grip, she laughed at the absurdity of his statement. She would never consider marrying a footman. It wasn't a situation of thinking herself better than him, it was more her father would never allow such a match and she didn't care for Collin in such a way. It was imprudent at best, ridiculous in the extreme, and would cause a scandal of the worst sort.

"You have high hopes for your future, Collin. But you will never take me as a wife. Not only because I will not accept you, but because my father will have you thrown into prison or shipped out to Barbados with the mere suggestion."

Scoffing at her statement, Collin's face contorted in anger. "Ashby has power, but he does not have the ability to ship me off to Barbados."

"Ask my brother Phillip what Ashby does with servants he doesn't like. The last one, Thomas, was thrown on a ship and sent away without a second thought." She failed to mention Thomas was her father's illegitimate son and how he tried to poison Phillip, but those details hardly seemed necessary at the moment.

"Do not threaten me, Lottie." Never had she given a man permission to use her Christian name. If Lord Haughton decided to call her Lottie, she'd allow him, but Collin was not someone she cared to use such an informality.

"You will stay away from me. If you come near me again, if you use my Christian name again, I will have my father send you away. You will never be welcome on his properties again."

As though her words hurt his sensibilities, Collin suddenly changed tactics. "I know you are in love with me, you are blinded by Haughton's wealth and title. I may not be wealthy, but I will love you.

Once we are married, I will have your dowry and we will inherit a home as Lord Arundel and Lord Edward did."

Again, she was shocked at his assumptions. "What makes you certain of my dowry?"

"I have heard talk of it below stairs. Everyone knows this is why Lord Riley plans to marry you. He desires your dowry. We do not know the exact amount, but we believe it has to be near twenty thousand pounds. If you inherit the home near London, Watson Manor, we will be near my family. They can live on the estate with us."

Disgusted by the plans he'd made and the conversations surrounding her dowry, Charlotte moved toward the doors. Before she left him standing by himself on the patio, she turned back to let him know there was no possibility he would win her hand and dowry. It was not the kindest way of refusing a man, but his expectations of marriage had to be stopped.

"I do not know why the serving staff believes my dowry and future are proper discussions, but I will make this very clear to you. I do not find you to be a suitable match. Your postulating on a marriage between us is not only ridiculous, but it is presumptive, and I will have no part in the matter. If you plan to remain in my father's service, you will keep your distance."

She marched up to her bedchamber and closed the door before allowing the stress of the confrontation to overwhelm her, sending her into tears. She was not one for confrontation, and the thought of speaking to a person in such a way was frightening. Allowing all the anger, hurt, and frustration of the evening out of her body, she threw herself on the bed and curled up with her pillow. She needed a hug but did not dare ask anyone to give her one for fear of having to reveal the terribly embarrassing conversation she'd just had with Collin. If she had any sort of strength, she'd ask her father to have him dismissed. But it would require an explanation, one she dared not give for fear of the assumption of having been ruined.

With the house party ending, Charlotte wished the footmen would leave as well. This would save her from another uncomfortable conversation with Collin, for she had a terrible feeling this wouldn't be the last.

Charlotte fell asleep without changing into her night clothes. By the time she woke the following morning, she was sore from her position and the tightness of her dress. Dreams of Collin and Haughton dueling over her hand plagued her mind, causing a restless night. Exhausted, she dressed for the day and found her way down to breakfast.

The house party ended with the previous day's activities. Originally, her mother wanted to have a ball, but it didn't seem right to have one with Lord Haughton so injured. Instead, they had a quiet evening of cards and conversation to end the four-week party. Hoping the guests were gone, Charlotte entered the dining room to find Lord Riley in conversation with her father. *Why am I not surprised!* Exasperated with the man and his insistence on admiring her, Charlotte found a spot at the end of the table as far away as she could from both men.

She ate slowly, as she knew Riley wanted to speak with her. She would have to give him the same speech she gave Collin the night before. *What do I say to that insufferable man?* While she ate, she prepared a new speech.

I do not have a desire to marry you. She buttered her toast as the words went through her mind. *Should I say them with vigor? If I say the word desire, will he fixate on it or will he hear the rest of my words?* Taking a bite of the toast, she slowly chewed while considering the options. *What if I say, "You are a cad, Lord Riley. Leave at once or I will set my brothers after you"?* The words made her smile as she sipped her tea. Phillip, Edward, and Charles would send him packing as fast as his horse would carry him.

I would never consider you for a match, you are too much of a rake. The thought made her cringe as she considered saying the words to him. Had she previously called him a rake? *He would take it as a compliment, insufferable man!* Charlotte took another sip of tea. Eating too much more would cause her indigestion during the confrontation. A few bites of toast were more than enough for this morning.

Before she could plan her recitation, Riley stood before her. "Lady Charlotte, might I have a moment of privacy with you?"

Without looking at him, she lifted her cup of tea and sipped one last time. Her mind muddled all the possible things she planned to say. Instead, she found her voice and set him in his place. "There is no need, my lord. May your journey land you in a ditch."

The intake of breath around the room brought her a moment of satisfaction, and then guilt settled. She didn't like Lord Riley, but the indifference didn't need to wish him injured.

"If this is how you feel, I will be on my way."

Sighing at her imprudent words, she apologized. "I should not have said such an unkind statement, my lord. I do hope your journey is safe, but no I will not speak with you in private."

With both of the annoying men in her life now offended by her brash words, Charlotte found her appetite returned as the smell of eggs made her stomach growl.

Chapter 23

"You will be eating in the dining room tonight," Doctor Moore informed Garrett.

"Why?"

"Your parents have requested you join them."

"Who else will be there? The entire party?" He tried to hold in the bitterness as he spoke. He didn't understand the demand to eat with everyone else. He knew they'd stare at him. He would have stared at a blind person if given the opportunity before the accident.

"No, only the residents of Wentworth Hall and your fiancé's family remain. The house party ended."

This was a surprise to Garrett. He'd known there was another card evening, as he'd refused to attend. How was he expected to enjoy a night of games without sight? "Did the party end early?"

"No, my lord."

"Have I really been out of touch with everyone for so long?"

"Yes, my lord. But you have made progress."

"Does the Duke of Ashby plan to leave for London? Will my family be forced to leave Wentworth Hall?"

"I do not know what is planned, my lord, but you will have to leave once you and Lady Ruby are married. Your parents want you to be married from Cholmondeley Hall. You will go home at some point."

Garrett knew the doctor spoke the truth, but was he ready to eat in the dining room with everyone else? Was he ready to leave the safety of his bedchamber?

Consigned to the demands of his father, he decided it would be a perfect time to speak about giving the title and inheritance to his brother. He'd decided on a new approach.

"How long do I have to prepare?"

"You are to dress now."

"Now?"

"Yes, my lord, and due to the need to hurry and to the importance of dressing for company, I will allow your valet to assist you."

"A happy thought indeed. I have not had a properly tied cravat for the whole of our acquaintance." Garrett rolled his useless eyes as the doctor chuckled. Even when sighted he'd never been expected to dress without a valet.

Dressing with help made him thankful he'd been born to privilege. For a fleeting moment, he wondered if he could fulfill his duties as Marquess with help from servants. Trusted servants. With this positive thought, he walked with as much dignity as he could, one hand on the doctor's shoulder, down to the parlor to meet with everyone before going into the dining room.

"Lord Haughton!" He did not know who spoke to him. It could be either Duke Ashby or Duke Dudley. Being blind is more difficult when outside the comfort of a bedchamber. "Duchess Ashby and I were hoping you would join us for dinner this evening. You must continue to leave the self-imposed seclusion you are so dedicated to keep."

"Yes, your grace." It was kind of him to mention a title, so he knew who was speaking. He noted the gruff tone in Ashby's voice so he wouldn't be confused in the future.

"Garrett, you will escort me through tonight," his mother said taking his arm and kissing his cheek.

It was an uncomfortable entrance. He knew everyone was doing their best to put him at ease, but the tension was thick. He allowed his mother to lead him into the dining room, which was an intimidating venture. Starting with soup wasn't difficult, but was he eating too fast or too slow? Courage building from not spilling any soup down his front, he moved onto the next course. Everyone around him spoke about their day and seemingly mundane tasks, none of it had any meaning to him.

Insecurity, anger, fear, anxiety, doubt, and many more emotions ran through him as he continued to take the fork from plate to mouth in each round of dinner, until he realized a large slice of meat sat before him. Taking a deep breath, Garrett found the knife and fork and sliced it. Worry immediately plagued him as he realized the piece he cut was far too large to be appropriate.

Taking the meat back down to his plate he tried to cut it again. This time the piece was so small there was hardly anything on his fork. *This is why I eat alone.* Moving to another spot on the plate, he found turnips. He did not like turnips but forced the bit he'd put in his mouth down. Giving up, he placed his silverware on the plate to indicate he was finished. *I have no desire to make a fool of myself in front of two dukes, an earl, and my fiancé.*

"Are you finished, my lord?" Garrett leaned to the side so the footman could take his plate.

"Yes."

He cringed as the doctor's voice rose over the quiet conversations. "Lord Haughton is not finished with this round. Put the plate back."

Tension filled the room. Garrett stiffened and held back his angry retort.

"Doctor, you will force Haughton to eat when he does not desire it? Can you work this same wonder with Arundel?" Edward said with a laugh.

"Edward!"

He didn't know who did the chiding, but it made everyone in the room laugh. Everyone except Garrett. He wondered if Arundel was laughing. It was a possibility, as Arundel and Edward were twins and they seemed to never get angry with the other.

"Put the plate back. Make certain the meat is situated at five o'clock."

"Yes, doctor."

This time Garrett didn't lean to the side for the footman. He stayed straight and still as he waited for the meal to finish. As time passed, Duchess Ashby excused the women from the room and Duke Ashby took the men through for their chatting. Deciding he'd prefer to spend the evening in his bedchamber, Garrett moved to find his way but was stopped by the doctor's voice.

"I will keep you here all night if you do not eat."

Certain they were alone, he finally lost his temper. It might have been juvenile to behave in such a way, but he was upset and embarrassed by his inability to cut the meat properly. "I do not appreciate you parading me around to show how far I have come in this process."

Pushing away from the table, he knocked the plate into the glass and heard the resulting break.

The doctor sighed in irritation. "You will need to straighten the table as well."

"I am not a servant." He'd never said such vile words. Although born to wealth, he'd never treated servants abominably. Even the memory of the words bothered him within seconds of saying them.

"You may not be a servant, but you made a mess. You also drenched your venison in wine, which will make for a cold soggy dinner."

Before he picked his plate from the table, he had a momentary thought of acquiescing to the doctor's desires. He could ask for a new slice of meat and eat the meal. It would be ridiculous to deny him a hot non-soggy piece of meat. Instead of heeding the internal warning, he tossed the plate over his shoulder.

"I will not eat this. You parade me down here and expect me to eat in a pleasing manner when I cannot even cut my meat to a correct size." The words came out as a hiss of anger. "Would you prefer me to eat with my hands?"

"You were taught table manners in your youth. You know how to cut meat."

"Do you have a book of these inspirational thoughts? If so, I would request a refund. You sit there with your eyesight staring at me while I try to function in the dark. You have watched me trip over my own feet, chairs, and little bumps on the path. I have fallen down the stairs more than I would like to admit with a newly healed leg, yet you continue to tell me I am not applying myself because these are simple tasks." In his built-up anger every little thing the doctor had said or done during the learning process came out in a rush. Garret's frustration came out with finally admitting, "I cannot see anything."

Turning to leave the room, he tripped over the chair next to him and crashed to the ground. His hand fell onto the venison he'd thrown only moments before and slipped forcing him to fall and hit his head.

In his stunned anger he registered arms around his waist.

"Stop helping him. If you do everything for him, he will never learn to function on his own."

"Do you expect me to watch my son struggle to get up from the ground?" Surprised by his father's voice, Garret slipped again on the venison. If his father was there, who else sat watching?

"Lord Cholmondeley," Doctor Moore said in a calm voice, "you hired me to teach your son how to function in a dark world. He has started to break free of the fear, but if you do everything for him, he will close up and never leave his bed again."

Garrett wanted to cry as his father moved away from him. "Father!" he called out, reaching his hand to find the comfort of the man who raised him. After a few minutes of finding no one, he tried to pull himself off the floor, but tripped again on the chair.

"Find your way out from the obstacle of the chair." Doctor Moore sounded bored.

Crippled with fear, Garrett sobbed out, "Father, please help me."

When a response didn't come, he crawled forward on the floor and hit into another obstacle. Pain shot through his side as he scraped what he could only guess was another chair.

"Lord Haughton," Doctor Moore said from only a few feet away, "did you count your steps as you entered the room?"

His mother's voice interrupted his curt response. "Doctor, this is not working."

"Mother, please help me get back to my chambers." She would not leave him on the floor. Counting on her love for him, he reached in the direction of her voice.

"Do not go near him."

The doctor's high-handed attitude with his parents enraged him. Again, his anger took over and he said things he'd never dreamed of thinking. "You are a lowly doctor. They are a Marquess and Marchioness, how dare you tell them what they can and cannot do?"

"I am doing my job."

Garrett pulled himself off the ground and hoped he was walking in the right direction for the door to the hall when he slammed into one of the banquet tables. He went down with the plates of excess food as he swore loudly. He was stuck in a nightmare without an end.

Finally, his mother came to his aid. She helped him up from the floor and the mess of food. Her arm guided him back to where he'd walked from, he was certain of it, and helped navigate around the mess.

"Where are you going?" He stilled with the doctor's words.

"To my bedchamber."

"You will clean the mess you have made before you retire."

"I am not a servant!" he repeated.

The doctor spoke deliberately as he said, "You will not eat again until you clean this room."

Before he walked out the door with his mother, he turned back to the doctor. "It will be a cold day in hell before I clean this mess."

As they entered the hall, he heard the doctor's reply to the Marquess. "I know it is hard to believe, but this is an improvement from what I have seen over the last weeks."

"Improvement! You cannot be serious," Cholmondeley yelled.

As they reached the stairs, he heard the doctor's response. "He must be pushed."

"You pushed too far."

Garrett tripped up the stairs as he was not concentrating. His mother kept hold of him, guiding him to his room. When he was in the safety of the space, he knew so well, his father and valet helped him wash and dress for bed.

Chapter 24

Thoughts of dinner plagued her as she tried to sleep. Ruby worried she wouldn't be up to the challenge of having an invalid for a husband. Her father continued to believe as long as he was heir to the marquess, Garrett was the only man he'd give her to.

Even though it'd only been a short time since he left, she longed to see Lord Madden. Longed to be near him and have him steal kisses from her.

With thoughts of Madden, she drifted into a restless slumber. The next morning, tired and in a foul temper, Ruby decided she would discuss the engagement with Haughton. *He cannot expect me to marry him. Not in this condition. There will have to be changes if we are to stay engaged.*

Listing the conditions in her mind, she made her way to Lord Haughton's sitting room. *First, he must come out of his bedchamber every day. Second, he will dress for the day instead of staying in night clothes. Third, he will not be allowed to have a temper. Fourth, I am tired of his self-absorbed attitude. He will need to think of me at times.* Listing these items in her mind, she repeated the words to become comfortable with her arguments. Slipping into the sitting room, she decided this was where he would need to meet with her. As she entered, she noticed the door to his bedchamber was open. In an effort to stave off ruin, she moved to close the door when she heard his voice.

"Nate, will you pen a letter for me?"

"Will the doctor approve? He tends to prefer you do things for yourself."

"I do not care."

Ruby thought about the rudeness of eavesdropping but decided it wouldn't hurt. He was to be her husband, after all.

"Certainly, my lord. Do you want me to use a specific paper?"

"No, the paper at my desk will be fine."

After a short pause, Nate responded, "I am ready, my lord."

Again, she thought about closing the door, but curiosity took over. She decided it would not hurt to listen. Someone else would soon be reading it. Convincing herself to stay, she settled against the wall.

"Dear Father and Mother, out of respect for you and my siblings, I have made every attempt to learn how to function without my sight."

The valet cleared his throat in a very loud and pretentious way.

"Do you disagree with me, Nate?" Haughton sounded irritated, which made Ruby smile.

Ruby disagreed. His behavior at dinner the night before was juvenile. He should have made every effort to eat when the doctor told him to. *Cutting meat is not so difficult.*

"Of course not, my lord. I had a frog in my throat."

"Very well . . . continue to write."

Haughton paused for a moment and Ruby again considered the impropriety of her behavior. Eavesdropping was frowned upon by her parents. Would she experience guilt for her actions? Turning to leave, she stopped with his next words.

"I cannot continue to disgrace you by pretending to be happy with my life. I am engaged to a woman I have no desire to marry. I did not ask for her hand, but as father has said, the situation is by the by."

Ruby wanted to stomp into his bedchamber and give him a piece of her mind, but he continued to speak.

"I have tried to speak with father on multiple occasions of my concerns regarding the title and inheritance. I cannot pretend to think any longer of being the marquess when father passes from this existence. The duties and expectations are beyond my current abilities, and I do not see anything changing as I am incapable of learning to live with this imperfection."

Hope surged in Ruby. If he were able to convince the marquess to make the younger son the heir over Haughton her father would demand the engagement be ended. Now she had leverage. She could reveal this information to her father, and they could get ahead of the disgrace of ending the engagement before a decision was made on the heir.

Haughton continued to speak. She missed a bit of his letter due to the planning she'd started. She nearly walked away when she heard the words, "Do not blame yourselves. You tried as best you could to help me during this difficulty and I appreciate you. My life should have ended when the horse spooked. I cannot pretend to feel hope. I feel a great sense of loss and loneliness."

Ruby put a hand over her mouth to stop the shriek from escaping. *He plans to*—even voicing the thought in her head was too much for her. Rushing from the sitting room, she ran to find Marquess and Marchioness Cholmondeley. They would put an end to this plan of his. Even if she had to marry him, she would prefer it to having him die by his own hand.

Running into the dining room she called out without thinking about who was in the room. "He is planning to end his life."

"Ruby, please do not yell unintelligible words at us," her mother said while spreading jam on toast. The calm in her voice only proved to urge Ruby to nervousness.

"Please, believe me. I went to see Lord Haughton and he asked his valet to write a letter. He said something about having a loss of hope and not seeing a way out of the situation as he is lonely, and I am certain he said he has melancholia. I have not a doubt he plans to end his life."

With the end of her speech, Lord and Lady Cholmondeley rushed from the room. Ruby sat on a chair and cried.

"He does not want to be the Marquess of Cholmondeley when the time comes. He wants to let his brother be the heir." Turning to her father she finished, "You will not want me to marry him if he is not the heir."

"Do not speak such drivel. It would be scandalous for Cholmondeley to name the younger son as heir while the elder lives." Her father's response was lazy.

She had to wonder what Duke and Duchess Ashby thought of the guests in their home. Her family remained due to her engagement to

Haughton. Haughton's family remained because of his condition. But they would need to leave soon, as the season was open and fashionably late was nearing its end.

Chapter 25

Ruby was not his favorite person, especially since she'd eavesdropped and misunderstood his plan. When listening in on a conversation, it was best to capture the entire situation before making an assumption. Trying to explain to a hysterical mother the decision to spend his life in a solitary cottage with a few servants to help him while she thought he planned suicide was a disaster.

Ending the engagement was at the forefront of his mind. He'd spent time thinking about the letter Nate penned for him. Garrett was anything but a coward. In truth, he knew he could never take his own life. The thought of his body in the ground was too much to bear while stuck in the dark.

The despair he currently experienced was not only due to the misunderstanding, but it was more that he was blind and an invalid. Since the fateful dinner where he'd made a complete fool of himself, he hadn't left his bedchamber. It was a rare day when he'd allow his father and valet to pull him from his bed to dress just so he'd sit in a chair in front of a window where he couldn't see the light.

As he considered his mood for the day and his decision to end the engagement with a scandal, his father entered his room and pulled him from his bed without allowing an argument. "Nate help him dress. Bring him to the parlor when he is ready."

"Father, I do not want to be out of bed today."

"I will hear no argument, Haughton. Be in the parlor within a quarter of an hour, or I will return for you and drag you down the stairs."

His father's tone told him he'd find no satisfaction in an argument. Since his parents stopped what they thought was a suicide plan, his father had been cold. His mother stayed away, as though ignoring him was his punishment. What they didn't know was the blindness was his punishment and he would live with it forever. Unlike the times he'd been censored as a child, the results of his actions would never go away. Reminding them he hadn't planned such an action didn't help. They ignored his comments and acted as though the plan to live a quiet life in a cottage away from everyone in society was tantamount to the same.

Acquiescing to his father's demands, he dressed and allowed the valet to comb his hair before leading him to the parlor. Each step closer to the room made him fear what his father had planned. It had to be serious. Cholmondeley was not one for theatrics.

"Haughton, I am surprised you found your way down here so quickly." His father was improvising. It was obvious by the tone and distance he stood from Garrett.

Deciding he wanted the truth, Garrett responded, "I have never known you to be so dramatic, father. Tell me you have considered my request for a quiet cottage so I can return to my solitude."

"You will not return to a bedchamber."

"Then where shall I go? Are you sending me back to Cholmondeley Hall? Or perhaps you can seclude me in one of the country estates you and mother rarely visit?" It was not fair for him to be so angry with his parents. They had every right to scold him for his actions. But after days of avoiding him, he finally had a chance to speak.

"You will return to Cholmondeley Hall."

"Am I to go alone?" The thought frightened him, but he didn't want his father to notice.

Cholmondeley cleared his throat in an uncomfortable moment. "No, you will not be alone."

"I thought you need to be in town for the opening of Parliament."

"I am going to London." Cholmondeley again cleared his throat.

"You are sending mother with me? I cannot protect her if something happens."

"No, your mother will accompany me to town."

"Then you are leaving me to the care of my valet?"

The room was silent as his father delayed in answering his question. As he was ready to ask again, his father put a hand on Garrett's shoulder. "Doctor Moore will accompany you to Cheshire. He will stay with you until you complete the lessons."

"So, I am to go back to school? I thought I was free of such institutions when I left Oxford."

His father sighed. It was a sound of exhaustion. "You will join us in London when you have completed your training."

Attitude hadn't changed his father's mind, so perhaps pleading would. "Father," his voice broke as he held his hand out, hoping it was in the direction his father stood, "please do not abandon me."

"I am helping you."

"Does mother know you are sending me away?"

"Yes, and I support your father in this decision." Who else stood or sat in the room to witness his embarrassment?

Garrett closed his useless eyes. It was a learned reaction from when he was sighted. "Who else is here?"

Ignoring the question, his father responded, "The carriage is waiting out front. You will leave now. I will have your valet pack your trunk and he will follow this afternoon."

Losing his composure, Garrett's emotions took over. "Please do not send me away. I beg of you. If this is because I asked for the title to be passed to James, it is an unfair punishment."

"Stop, Garrett, we are past these emotional pleadings." His father took hold of his arm. "I will walk with you to the carriage."

Without so much as a farewell, Garrett was forced into the carriage with the doctor and sent away. *Perhaps this is best*, he thought as the carriage drove toward his family home. *No one will have to look at me and pity me if I am out of sight.* This was essentially what he had requested. Although Cholmondeley Hall was massive and finding his way around would take much more effort. He entertained thoughts as they drove, his mind delving into the dark self-pity he'd been distracted with over the past weeks. By the time they arrived at their destination, Garrett was tired, angry, and ready to be on his own.

Doctor Moore didn't allow him to sleep late. His mornings were filled with everything from relearning to feed himself to walking the house and land to familiarize himself with it. He agreed with the doctor, it was nice to be able to find his way around a house. Since he'd grown up at Cholmondeley Hall, it was a place he remembered and the process was easier than it had been at Wentworth Hall.

Since he had no sense of time, he woke without knowing if it was morning or night. Able to dress himself, thanks to the doctor, he made his way down to the stables. Nate told him that Cholmondeley had sent Sun Dancer back to Cheshire soon after the accident. It'd been far too long since he'd visited the horse.

As he entered the stables, he ignored the surprised noises from the servants and made his way to Sun Dancer's stall. Rubbing the horse's muzzle, he finally felt whole. He'd missed his horse.

"I'm sorry it's taken me so long to visit you," he said putting his forehead against the horse's. "I do not blame you for what happened." It never crossed his mind to blame the horse as no one knew how the accident occurred. "I will visit you more often." He'd make regular trips out to the barn now he knew he could find his way.

He'd thought over the accident numerous times. If he'd taken the day differently, the accident wouldn't have happened. Staying with the group during the hunting party would have saved him a great deal of stress. If he hadn't kissed Charlotte, he wouldn't have had the need to speak with Arundel and Edward. But the worst part was he had no clear memory of the accident, and it bothered him.

Counting his steps as he walked back to the house, Garrett stopped as he realized his eyes hurt. This time it wasn't from lack of use, as they'd often pained him the weeks following the accident. The pain he currently had was a need to shield his eyes from the sun. He walked further into the house before he realized the implications of light bothering his eyes.

Excitement and relief guiding his decisions, he called out, "Jeffries!" His eyes attempting to adjust to his surroundings made him dizzy. It wasn't easy to walk, and he still had to rely on his cane and counting as depth perception unnerved him. *Is the floor truly so far down?* "Jeffries, where are you?"

The butler rushed out to the hall as Garrett yelled his name. "My lord, is there something amiss?"

"Where is Doctor Moore?"

"Breakfasting."

Turning to go back to the dining room, Garrett knocked over a large vase. Crashing to the ground his eyes again attempted to focus. They were blurry at best, but he could see light. He could see the mess he'd made and the butler helping him from the floor. Large items were blurry, but easier to make out.

"What happened?" Doctor Moore asked rushing from the dining room. "Are you injured?"

"No, but I do not think my mother will ever forgive me for breaking this particular vase. It has been in the family for generations." Far too excited about his eyes, he almost burst with the news when the doctor spoke again.

"You should not be so careless. Have I not taught you to count your steps? Have I not taught you to use the wall for guidance while walking?"

The doctor's frustration was finally voiced. There had been other moments, like during the final dinner at Wentworth Hall that had made Garrett wonder about the doctor's temper, but after so many weeks of doing well with the lessons, it was a shock. Also, he had wonderful news to share as this could be the beginning of healing.

"I received a letter from your parents. They want you in London. Do you think you can handle learning a new house without destroying more family heirlooms?"

Again, he wanted to tell the doctor about his eyesight, but the doctor's overreaction stopped him. The doctor's sharp rebuke made him less confident in confiding. "Is there a reason they want me in London so soon? We have only been here a month."

Doctor Moore looked down at the paper in his hand. Garrett made an effort not to follow him with his eyes. It wasn't difficult for his eyes to stay still, as they hadn't needed to move in months. It was more following with his head he feared would give him away.

"The marquess speaks about your engagement and the need to discuss it with you."

"I am surprised he wants me in London. Can he not make the trip to Cheshire?"

"We are to depart today."

Garrett did not like Doctor Moore. The man was difficult and unfeeling, especially when it came to Garrett's struggles. Confiding his renewal of eyesight could happen when he arrived in London. He would speak to his parents about it.

The trip was long and tedious as usual, and there were times he wished they'd stayed at Cholmondeley House, but when they rolled into London, the trip was worth it. Garrett spent most of the time looking out the window. He'd done the same thing on his ride from Wentworth Hall to Cheshire with only the dark to entertain him. After a few months of darkness, the landscape was something he wanted to witness and see even if it was patches with a big blur. He would never take his eyesight for granted again once it fully returned.

But, the continued pretense of not letting the doctor know of his healing was difficult to hide. At each stop, Nate helped him down from the carriage and allowed him to hold onto his shoulder. Garrett appreciated the valet more and more as he realized the burden he'd placed upon everyone around him.

This realization hadn't come until his eyes started to heal, which not only gave him an insight into those around him, but also into himself. He'd been insufferable and spoiled. He vowed to change and be a better person.

As Kensington House came into view, he had to stop himself from smiling. It would be too obvious if he knew they'd arrived.

"We are at your family house, my lord."

Without looking at the doctor, Garrett responded, "Thank you."

His father rushed out to the carriage and helped him down. He knew it was the man who raised him by the short rotund figure in front of him. Again, a pang of guilt went through him, but it wasn't for the help his father was giving him, it was now for the blurred pity he saw in his father's expression. Cholmondeley told him more than once he was not pitied, but from what he currently saw, those words were not the truth.

His mother had the same expression, as did his sisters and younger brother. In a very unwise, split-second decision, he chose to continue the charade. He would remain blind until he knew exactly what his family and Ruby thought of his condition. He would not marry a woman who pitied him and was only staying in the engagement for money. But it was also easy to rationalize the deception for everything remained blurry. Perhaps he'd need spectacles, but he could handle such a development if it meant he could see again.

Chapter 26

Charlotte refused to admit her heartbreak after crying to her sisters. She was over it. Over Lord Haughton. He chose Ruby over her, and although Ruby was not in love with him, there was no way to change the situation.

After a week in London, Charlotte decided she would make this the season to find a husband by putting in more effort than she had any other year. She'd replace her wardrobe and spend the season flirting and dancing. She would forget Lord Haughton and the kisses he stole from her. She planned to forget the summer house party ever happened.

Instead of standing bored on the sides of ballrooms hoping to blend into the drapery, Charlotte told her brothers to introduce her to all of their friends. After a month of introductions, she was tired. She'd found their friends were nice, but none of them measured up to Haughton.

Standing on the sidelines of Lord and Lady Wyndoms' ballroom and distracted by Charles and Lillian, she didn't notice much going on. She wondered if they were just friends or interested in courting. Charlotte watched as they danced and wished she were just starting her first season. Wishing she could go back in time and find Lord Haughton before Ruby entered society, she caught herself and chided, *Do not think of Haughton!*

Seeing movement to the side, Charlotte turned as Phillip approached with another man. *Smile, be pleasant, try to fall in love.*

"Lord Branton, this is my sister Lady Charlotte."

Handsome, yes. Kind, yes. But was he Lord Haughton . . . no. Not anywhere near Lord Haughton's caliber. *Do not compare him to Haughton! No one will measure up.*

Phillip continued, "Charlotte, Lord Branton is the eldest son of Duke and Duchess Wymount."

"Lady Charlotte, I asked Arundel to introduce me so I could pull you away from the drapery and entice you to dance."

"Thank you, my lord, I would love to dance." Of course her response was the right one, but she didn't want to dance with him. *If I am to find a husband, I need to be more agreeable!*

Standing next to the other people on the dance floor, she smiled and forced herself to enjoy the conversation. Lord Branton could be funny and kind. The thought was a disappointment for her because although the goal was to find a husband, she didn't want to move past Lord Haughton.

"Have you enjoyed the season?" Lord Branton asked. It wasn't an overly exciting conversation starter. Most men asked her the same thing. *Is it too much to ask to have an interesting man? Interesting conversation? How can my brothers associate with such boring men?*

"Yes, Lord Branton." In an effort to take the conversation away from the mundane, she asked, "Tell me, what is the last book you read?"

"Are you a blue stocking?" He quirked an eyebrow to show he was teasing her.

Charlotte laughed far too loud for the room and occasion. "No, my lord, but I do plan to judge you based on your choices in literature."

He quirked his perfect eyebrow again and smiled broadly. "I last read this interesting little adventure called *Gulliver's Travels*. I must admit it was more pleasant than I expected."

"I have not read it."

"Tell me, Lady Charlotte, what was the last book you read?"

"*Robinson Crusoe*."

She turned in the dance and came back around for the finish. Lord Branton looked nervous as to where to take the conversation. But she was pleasantly surprised by his next question.

"Please tell me the conclusions you made based on my decision to enjoy Mr. Swift's creation?"

"The choice to enjoy Mr. Swift's world tells me you are brilliant and imaginative. You enjoy the unknown and prefer fiction to reality."

"Continue to say such things, my lady, and you might make me blush."

Charlotte liked his witty banter, especially when he asked, "Are you not curious to know my judgments of you based on Robinson Crusoe?"

She smiled and gave him a flirtatious glance. "Please amuse me, and perhaps I will deign to confirm or deny your assumptions."

It was now his turn to laugh louder than necessary. The other dancers looked toward them, some men raising their eyebrows as though they were interested in the conversation as she hadn't been as lively with them. She knew there would be gossip but didn't care. Lord Branton was turning out to be a better companion than she'd originally imagined.

"Mr. Defoe's book would draw readers interested in adventure. You are resourceful, clever, and quick witted. And, might I add, beautiful beyond belief."

Charlotte's cheeks went instantly pink. "I do believe you said that only to see me blush."

"I have been wicked. Please forgive me."

As the dance ended, he walked her back to her mother. "It has been a pleasure, my lady."

"As for me."

"Will you join me for a ride in Hyde Park tomorrow?"

She gave her most alluring smile and agreed to the trip. *Perhaps,* she thought, *Lord Branton might be the diversion I am looking for to make me forget Lord Haughton.*

By the following week, Charlotte had more admirers than she expected and two she didn't want. Along with all the London admirers, Lord Riley joined the group congregating in the morning room each day and Collin was the other unwanted admirer. If she'd told her father the moment Collin declared himself, it would have been best. After months of keeping silent, she feared Ashby would see it as compliance and acceptance of Collin's declaration. For this reason, she dared not mention anything to him, which meant she had to endure Collin's subtle hints.

Her flirtatious smile, new dresses, and witty attitude pulled men to her like bees to honey. Dressing with care, as she expected to spend her evening flirting with Lord Branton, Charlotte found a shock upon entering Kingston house to see Lord Haughton. The last information she'd had was that he was still in Cheshire.

Distracted by his presence, she watched as he stood on the outskirts of the room speaking with anyone who approached. He held a cane and, although it was in style, it was merely the result of blindness. Charlotte knew it would only cause her stress to speak with him, but she needed to know how he fared. Just looking at him across the room made her nervous. While Branton and her admirers spoke and danced with other women, she decided it was time to make the effort of speaking with him. Shaking as she walked, she crossed the room and out of habit curtsied. He only bowed after she spoke.

"Lord Haughton, you look well." Hoping he knew who she was, without having to announce her name, she continued, "I am surprised to see you in London. I thought you in Cheshire all this time."

"I arrived two days ago, my lady."

Unable to tell from his words if he recognized her voice, she hesitated.

"Lady Charlotte," he said, his face looking past her to the rest of the room. She wished he would look at her, then remembered he was blind. It did not matter. "I have desired to speak with you. But I worry we would be overheard in here."

"It is a bit warm, my lord, if you would allow me to assist you out to the patio we can speak there."

Haughton nodded. She took his arm and led him from the crowded ballroom. As the cool evening air hit, she took a deep breath. Dancing for most of the evening had caused her to be a bit overheated. The cool air was a relief.

They walked to the edge of the patio and stood against the cement railing. Haughton closed his eyes before speaking to her. "I owe you an apology."

"I already told you it was not necessary."

"I know. But I have a feeling you and everyone else have extended the curtesy of forgiveness for my behavior due to the accident."

"How could we not?" It was a terrible response. For a moment she wondered if he could see her due to the way his lips turned up at her words, but realized it was ridiculous. If his eyes were healed, he would have said something.

"Are you telling me everyone pitied me?"

Charlotte sighed. "I think there are some who do. But only because they love you."

"Do you pity me?"

Charlotte knew looking him in the face didn't matter, but she wanted to see his eyes. "No, my lord, I do not pity you."

"Then why do you refuse to allow an apology? I used you."

Charlotte turned to ensure they were alone. It would not do to have someone listen in on their conversation. "I have a confession . . . I did not swoon when you kissed me." She whispered just in case there was a lurker. His insistence at clearing the air between them brought back the guilt of her foolish actions.

Haughton laughed. Looking amused he asked, "You have carried the guilt all these months?"

"Yes, I have." She put as much of an apology in her cringe as she could muster.

"Tell me, Lady Charlotte, why did you fake a swoon?"

Thankful he could not see her blush, she answered, "You are engaged. It was wrong."

Haughton nodded. "Ruby does not care for me."

"How do you know?"

"Blindness changes your senses. I learned to identify from a person's voice how they feel about me."

"And what do you interpret from my voice?" Asking the question made her blush again. Such a shocking and scandalous question.

"You are happy. You have moved past me."

Again, thankful he didn't have the ability to see her facial expressions, she frowned. "Should I be pining for you?"

From his reaction, she again questioned his inability to see. But the doubt crept back in. He would never cause his family such distress if it weren't true.

"Charlotte," he said reaching out to her. His eyes focused on her for the first time since they'd started speaking. "I did not kiss you with malicious intent. I kissed you because I was confused. I never offered for Ruby's hand, and my emotions were . . . addled."

Charlotte gave a little laugh and shook her head. "I cannot tell you how long I have waited to be told I was kissed due to addled and confused emotions." She held in a rush of tears threatening to spill at the confession. "I hope you do not hold it against me if I leave you out here."

"No, I do not mind. I was tired of the insincerity of my parents' friends."

Walking away from him, she rushed to the lady's lounge to freshen up and calm her nerves. She would need her wits if she were to dance with Lord Branton. She checked her hair, pinched her cheeks to bring out the pink, and let out a calming breath. *I can do this. I will have a proposal before the end of this season.* With this goal in mind, she set out for the ballroom.

"Lady Charlotte, you light up every room you enter," Lord Riley drawled, taking hold of her elbow.

"A fortunate attribute." She yanked her arm away from his grip and turned to go back into the lady's lounge. He wouldn't dare follow her in. Before she could go through the door, he took hold of her arm and dragged her down the hall.

"You will not walk away from me."

Charlotte tried to hit him but failed as he twisted her arm behind her back. She attempted to stomp on his foot, kick him, and give all manner of fight to his hold on her, but he was too strong for her smaller frame.

"What do you want from me?" she asked as he turned her to face him and pushed her against the wall.

"You will accept my proposal."

"I will do nothing of the sort."

Charlotte didn't want to cause a scene, as it would look negatively toward her. She would be considered a wanton who flaunted in front of men and tested their limits. In the end, the scandal would be on her, not Lord Riley.

"I will make you regret your decision."

He took hold of her face and forced her head up so she had to look him in the eyes. The pinch of his fingers caused her head and jaw to ache. She'd seen her father hurt her older brother the same way and knew a marriage with this type of man would be worse than death. As tears streamed down her cheeks, she cursed inwardly over her weakness, but the hold he had on her was painful.

Teeth clenched as though he exerted all the energy in his body, he whispered, "What is your answer?"

Unable to say much, as he tightened his hold on her jaw, she found her voice. It was more of a deep guttural groan from the back of her throat, but she croaked out the words. "I would prefer to die."

With the hold he had on her, it was not a ridiculous thought. The glint of anger in his eyes made her think he'd considered the possibility of killing her. Slamming her head against the wall, he laughed. She realized he was enjoying this moment of torture. Riley's hand closed tight around her neck, and she had the unpleasant thought of his dreadful face being the last she would see. Instead, she closed her eyes and thought of Lord Haughton. She thought of the conversation she'd had with him and remembered his face.

"Let her go." The words came to her from a distant tunnel. Haughton's voice was the last she heard. Stunned by the shocking manner in which Riley held her, she succumbed to the darkness as her eyes closed.

Chapter 27

His reasons for telling Charlotte a falsehood seemed right until he saw the tears in her eyes. The pretense of staying blind proved to be more difficult than he imagined. Many times over the past three days he thought it would be best to tell his parents, but now he did not know exactly how to tell them. So, he continued to be blind; although, he could excuse the deception away as there was blurriness still and the headaches he had from the sun were terrible.

Making the effort to act as though he needed help into the ballroom, he ran into his brother from behind.

"Where do you need to go?" James asked showing as much sympathy and pity as he could in his facial expression but forcing a jovial tone in his voice. He'd known fake people in the past, but never his family.

"Please help me back to my place against the tapestry."

As he walked, hand on James's shoulder, he used his eyes without turning his head to search for Lady Charlotte. He didn't see her, but her sister Marianne was speaking to a group of men. Charlotte would join her before too long. *She has every right to do so*, he reminded himself as jealousy formed in the pit of his stomach. A search for Ruby ended at the dancing. Paired with Lord Madden, again. *Is this their second or third dance of the evening?* He couldn't remember. Having a fiancé should be reason enough for her to abstain from dancing with the same man more than once.

The way Ruby looked at Madden made Garrett's blood boil. No, he didn't love Ruby. He'd realized this long before now. But she'd trapped him in an engagement and the least she could do would be to end it with him or flirt with him. At least try to look like she wanted to be Lady Haughton instead of Lady Madden. Although, flirting required energy and he currently didn't want to apply effort to Ruby.

The reason for his trip to London was to discuss the engagement. His father had yet to bring the subject to him. He wondered if he should do so, especially after Ruby's behavior. Standing on his own by the tapestry was boring and he tired of watching for Charlotte as she hadn't rejoined the people she'd been with earlier. Thinking of the attention surrounding her, he wondered how he could have been so blind before now.

He laughed to himself, it was ironic he asked such a question after months of physical and mental blindness. But to forget about the unbearable brat Ruby had been as a child merely due to beauty was a mystery to him. He never thought he had poor judgement until kissing Lady Ruby.

Bored with the evening, he touched his Aunt Grace's arm. She'd been placed on the chair next to his spot to help when needed.

"I want to retire for the evening. Will you guide me to the stairs?"

"Haughton, please stay a bit longer. Your father will be displeased with your early departure, especially due to this ball being in your honor."

He growled, "It may be so, but no one has spoken to me for most of the night. No one wants the uncomfortable experience of conversing with an invalid." Calming down he finished, "And I have a headache."

Taking his arm in hers, she helped him out of the room. "I understand, my dear boy." As she left him at the stairs, she kissed his cheek. "You do know we all love you?"

"Yes, dear aunt, and I adore you! Thank you for your assistance." Making sure to show thanks by kissing his aunt's cheek, he left for solitude.

"Do you need my help to find your chambers?" Her expression was one of love. Only the second person to show true compassion.

"I will be fine . . . but thank you for the offer."

He started up the stairs but heard a muffled squeak from the hallway. Looking around to see if anyone was watching, Garrett abandoned the stairs and moved down the hall. As he neared, he shook his head at the scene and thought it best to turn around and allow the couple to finish their discussion until he understood it wasn't two people in a romantic assignation, it was a struggle.

"Let her go!" he yelled, noticing Charlotte and the hold Riley had on her neck.

"Get out of it, Haughton. This does not concern you."

Charlotte's face was tear stained and red. Continuing his pretense of blindness seemed ridiculous as he needed to save her life. "I told you to release her."

"Take your walking stick and go back to the ballroom. This is a private matter."

Noticing her eyes gloss over, Garrett pulled his arm back, clenched his fist, and rammed it into Riley's jaw. The man staggered back as Haughton caught Charlotte in his arms.

Garrett yelled for help as he tried to wake her. Laying the unconscious lady on the floor, he looked up to face the culprit. "What did you do to her?"

"I do not answer to you, Haughton." Even with repairing eyesight, it was a surprise when Riley grabbed Garrett's cravat pulling him up from his position next to Charlotte. Riley's fist met Garrett's jaw before releasing him to the ground. The scuffle was too loud to not be overheard, which brought an audience and ended with another bump on Garrett's head and Riley escaping the scene. Garrett allowed his father to take Lady Charlotte as he carried her to a private room. His mother took his arm and without question guided him to the same area. This could be the moment he let people know his sight was back. His mother cleaned the wound on his head and when the doctor arrived, she forced him to allow the doctor to check him after taking a look at Lady Charlotte.

"Does your head hurt?" Doctor Bell asked. It was nice Ashby's physician traveled to London to be available when needed. Bell knew Garrett's history as he'd attended him after the accident at Wentworth Hall.

"I have experienced headaches of late." This would be the perfect opportunity to reveal the healing his eyes had done. Yet, he stayed silent.

Doctor Bell examined the bump on Garrett's head. When he pressed on the injury, Garrett winced from the pain. Pulling away from the doctor, Garrett put his hands on the pressure points of his head.

"Doctor," his Aunt Grace said, walking forward, "he had a headache only a short time ago."

She spoke the truth, although Garrett had hoped to escape the exam. Aunt Grace's words were used as a catalyst, Garrett's mother spoke of the few headaches he'd had since arriving in London. Although an adult, listening to the reports on his health made him feel like a naughty child.

Holding the candle up, the light shone directly into Garrett's eyes causing him to blink. *The deception is over.* It had to be over. The doctor would realize his eyes were healing.

"Can you see the light?" Doctor Bell asked, placing the candle on the table.

"My eyes have slowly been healing since I left Cheshire. Everything is blurry, but I can see light."

The intake of breath from both his parents was not a surprise. It had been wrong to keep this information from them. He thought about apologizing but decided to leave it until they were alone.

"It is possible you might need spectacles. I could recommend a specialist."

"I hope to have my eyes heal completely, Doctor. I do not plan to wear spectacles." It might be materialistic of him, but he had a difficult time imagining the addition to his face.

"Until you are healed, they could help you with navigation."

Garrett raised his eyebrows, "What good is all the learning I did to live in the dark, if I cannot function with partial sight?"

"Spectacles will also alleviate the headaches you are suffering."

"I highly doubt that, doctor, the headaches usually come after I have spent too much time in sunlight. I believe the pain is from the lack of light for so long."

"It is possible." The doctor seemed to consider his words as a legitimate reason for the pain. "Although I will suggest rest until your eyes further heal."

Not promising the doctor anything, Garrett took his mother's arm as she led him up to his room. It was an uncomfortable walk as he considered the depth of his deception. "Mother, will you forgive me for not telling you about my eyes?"

"I would like to know why you kept it a secret."

Considering his reasons for the rest of the walk, when she was about to leave him at his door he said, "I did not want to give false hopes to you and Father, but I also have had a difficult time accepting it myself and if I do accept it and my eyes do not improve, how can I handle the disappointment?"

His mother walked back to him and gave him an embrace. "I understand. But do not keep such information from us in the future."

This he could promise. He gave his word to her and made his way into the chambers to lie down. The headache he'd claimed earlier had come to fruition.

"Father?" Garrett asked as he entered the den. It was a relief not to have to pretend full blindness. "Is there any word on Lady Charlotte?"

"Come in." Cholmondeley rushed over to guide him to a chair.

"Lady Charlotte?" he asked again. He didn't want his father to change the topic.

"Resting. If Ashby catches Riley, well, I fear Riley will never stand trial for what he did. Ashby will take matters into his own hands."

It said a lot to him to realize this news was not disturbing. He loved Charlotte. When he'd seen her struggling for air, his mind went into preservation mode. But after a night of thinking on it, he thought of how she very well could have been found dead. The fear of this thought brought terrible nightmares and made his heart ache.

"She will stay here until this afternoon when Duke and Duchess Ashby arrive to take her home. It was best not to move her."

He remembered the doctor telling her parents to let her stay the night. It brought him comfort to know she'd be in the same house. Now he only wanted to see her. But what would he find? She would be bruised, no doubt.

"I wanted to speak with you, Garrett," his father continued. "It is about the confessions you made to me while at Wentworth Hall."

This caused Garrett to pull out of his thoughts. "Have you a solution?"

"I have asked Dudley and Ruby to visit today. I want to end the charade quickly and quietly. With you finding Lady Charlotte last night, there will be chatter among those in attendance, and it could ruin her reputation."

He had not considered such a drastic course. "I do not understand. I saved her life. I was not the one assaulting her."

"I know, but assault is how society will view the situation. Ashby is considering men who would willingly restore her reputation."

This last comment made him ill. Forcing the words from his mouth, he said, "A marriage?"

"Yes, and I know you would willingly marry her. I do not know if Ashby will accept the match, but if it is between his daughter's reputation and a match with my son, I think he will acquiesce."

"I do not want her to be forced, Father."

"Forced!" his father commented loudly and without humor. "That poor girl will be forced into a marriage. And it is better it is with you than someone similar to Riley, unless your feelings have changed."

"My feelings are unchanged. I am in love with Charlotte."

"I cannot promise Dudley will agree to end the engagement."

"Ruby is in love with Lord Madden." He hadn't yet revealed his memory of the assignation, as he wasn't certain it was real or a dream.

"How do you know?"

"Blindness heightens other senses. I have wonderful hearing, and it has been a topic of conversation since I woke at Wentworth Hall."

"I will discuss this with Dudley today."

"I wanted to explain why I kept the information regarding my eyes quiet." Knowing his mother would have shared the information with her husband, he still found the need to explain.

"No need to speak about it. Your mother and I discussed it long into the night."

Deciding it was best to leave, he stood, then remembered what his father said about Ashby and a possible match. "Father, why would Ashby oppose a match with your heir?"

"Do not worry about it." The backtracking in his voice made Garrett more curious.

"I thought you were on positive terms with Ashby."

"I am. It was an errant thought."

He wanted to ask further, but unfortunately Dudley and Ruby were introduced.

"Lord Haughton," Ruby's words echoed through his mind. This was the first time she'd addressed him since he'd left Wentworth Hall. She'd not even spoken to him the night before at the party.

Standing as was polite, he nodded to her and waited for Ruby to take a seat.

"We heard your sight is returning, Lord Haughton. This is a relief," Dudley said in a very unbelievable tone. His voice conveyed a sense of boredom.

"Thank you, your grace. I hope my eyes continue to heal."

"Now Haughton's healing, we should discuss the reading of the banns." Dudley continued speaking as though Garrett hadn't spoken and wasn't even a part of the conversation.

Continuing the pretense of the engagement was unnecessary. Ruby did not care for him, and she was obviously in love with Madden, or at least fancied him if it wasn't love. "I am asking to be released from the engagement, your grace."

"You would dishonor and ruin my daughter?"

"No. I would make certain everyone knows Ruby is the one who ended the engagement due to the shocking situation I saved Lady Charlotte from last night. I will also keep the assignation I witnessed at Wentworth Hall a secret, if I am freed from the agreement. Her virtue will be safe." It was a more than generous offer, he only hoped the memory was real.

"No, I do not agree with this solution. My daughter will remain your fiancé until the banns are finished." Dudley's angry retort bothered him. Looking to his father for help, it was a relief when Cholmondeley took his side.

"Let me tell you of your precious daughter, Dudley." Ruby looked down at her hands, and Garrett watched as her face turned pale at the implications his father threw out. He listened as his father spoke of rumors regarding Ruby and Madden. Between wanting to defend her and knowing the rumors had some portion of truth, Garrett stayed silent. "What do you have to say for yourself?" Cholmondeley asked. The room went silent as everyone waited for Ruby to speak.

"Lord Haughton, can you dance with me?" Her voice was barely above a whisper, but he could hear the tremor.

"Perhaps once my sight clears, but for now you know I cannot see properly to dance."

"Can you lead me into dinner and help me with my seat?"

"I do not have a problem helping you to your seat, but I would need assistance leading you into a room I am unacquainted with or filled with other people as long as my eyes are still compromised."

Ruby visibly swallowed before she finished, "Can you see me? Can you dote on me and tell me how lovely I look in a new dress or if my hair is lovely?

These compliments were important to Ruby. Sighted, yes, he'd be able to compliment her day in and day out. In his current state of partial blindness, it was not impossible, but he did not want to admit this. While he had been blind, he came to realize there was much more to a woman than her sparkling eyes and beautiful smile.

"I would admire you based off of moments with you." This was not a lie. He had no reason to think he'd want to pay compliment to her based off her current behavior even if she did dazzle him by wearing a new dress.

Ruby sniffed and wiped tears from her eyes. As a gentleman he pulled out a handkerchief and handed it to her. As a headache crept into the back of his head, he rubbed the side of his forehead to alleviate pain.

"I agree. I cannot marry you." Her words were barely heard above the sound of the clock on his father's desk. She looked frightened.

"Cholmondeley, my daughter deserves restitution for the ending of this engagement."

"Her weakness is not Garrett's fault."

"Father," Garrett said with great control, "please give a settlement so whatever this is can end."

His father looked at him with concern. Thankful there wasn't pity in his expression, Garrett stared forward, pretending his father's expression wasn't discernible.

"What amount do you think is appropriate, Dudley?"

Dudley looked ready to reject any offer of money until Ruby released another strangled whimper. "Five thousand pounds should be sufficient."

Without argument, his father agreed. "I will arrange for my solicitor to send the amount to you by the end of today."

Dudley stood as did Ruby. Could this part of the nightmare truly be over? Garrett stood out of habit yet hardly believed the fortune he had with the turn of events. Taking the full blame for the dissolution of their commitment didn't bother him.

"I wish you well, Lord Haughton." Ruby curtsied toward him as she said the words.

He nodded and in a genuine and kind desire for her he said, "As to you."

After they were gone, his father took hold of his arm. "Your mother said she would hold the morning meal for us."

Allowing his father to lead him out of the room, Garrett ate as he quietly contemplated when and how he would tell Charlotte of the situation with Ruby. He hoped she would accept his proposal. But as the meal progressed, his sister Lillian made an astute comment.

"Garrett, you can now find a woman who will love you and not your title and wealth. Someone like Lady Charlotte."

"What makes you believe she is in love with me?"

"The way she looks at you."

Garrett raised his eyebrows in surprise. "I will have to trust your observations."

"You have saved her from certain death twice over. How can she not love you?" Hazel said joining the conversation.

Garrett turned toward his mother. "How is Lady Charlotte? She has not left yet?"

"She will be able to go back to Lancaster house this morning. I had a tray sent up for her, and Duchess Ashby is already here to retrieve her."

This did not tell him in any certain terms how Charlotte fared. "So, she is well?"

"Yes, my dear, a vision of beauty this morning."

He ate, then followed his parents and sisters to the morning room as Ashby and Arundel arrived to escort Charlotte home. Garrett sat on the sofa, listening to the conversation about Riley. He didn't find a need to participate as he had nothing to offer that would add meaning.

"I never imagined Riley would turn out to be such a fiend," Ashby barked in frustration. He paced the room, which bothered Garrett's eyes. Quick movements tended to cause headaches, and if he watched Ashby much longer, he'd need to lie down.

"We owe you a debt of gratitude, Haughton." Arundel spoke from beside him. Garrett turned his entire head, although the movement didn't help the headache forming.

"There is no need to speak of it."

Ashby huffed, "What is taking so long? I have business this morning."

"Father, I will stay with mother to escort her and Charlotte home if you are otherwise engaged."

"No. No need to worry, Arundel." Ashby's grunt told everyone the exact opposite of his words was true.

"Charlotte," Arundel's voice expressed Garrett's horror at seeing Charlotte's bruised neck and face as she entered the room. Of course, it could be a trick of his compromised vision, but he was certain the bruises were in the shape of Riley's handprints.

"Lord and Lady Cholmondeley, I thank you for your hospitality." She looked to him. He wanted to react but schooled his features as no one else reacted with abhorrence. "Lord Haughton, I cannot thank you enough for your quick actions which preserved me."

He nodded and with much hesitation asked, "You are well?"

"Yes, very much so. There was no harm done."

"I am glad to hear." The handprints on her neck bothered him. He wished Riley had received the same treatment, but he'd been far too occupied trying to help Charlotte to chase after the man.

Garrett noticed her inattention to the conversation, and the way she constantly looked his way. Lillian was right, Charlotte did seem interested in him. Perhaps she hadn't moved past him as he'd thought. The joy he experienced with this thought nearly put a smile on his face. He wondered if she'd been informed of his sight partially returning, as it was far too early to celebrate perfect sight.

Taking him out of the thoughts occupying his mind, he heard Arundel ask, "We saw Dudley this morning. He informed us the engagement is off?"

"Yes," Garrett said before anyone else could answer, "Ruby chose to take time as she is young and does not need an invalid for a husband."

"As is the official story for society," Arundel said.

"It is the only story we are sharing," Cholmondeley said, stopping Garrett from divulging any confidences. He need not have worried. Garrett was serious when he promised to stay silent on the matter.

"Whatever the truth, both Edward and I were happy to hear the news." Arundel was a good friend, and perhaps one day Garrett would confide in him. But at this moment, it wasn't necessary.

Cutting over the conversation, Ashby laughed as he said, "Since this is true, you and Dudley will have a disadvantage with winning over me."

"What?" Garrett asked, turning toward his father.

Guilt covered his father's face. Even with the blurriness in his eyes he could see the flush in his father's skin. "It is nothing you need worry over, Haughton."

Knowing Ashby's talent for making irresponsible bets, he knew the effort behind discovering the details wouldn't be easy. Cholmondeley only ever entered into ill-advised gambles when he was around Ashby, and he always lost.

"There is no need to discuss this now, Ashby. We can meet at White's this evening for drinks and cards to fine tune the details of our arrangement.

"Ashby will not be there," Duchess Ashby said while glaring at her husband. "I cannot even imagine what you have done this time. We will discuss it on our way home."

Hiding his surprise at the duchess's words, he tried not to laugh as he thought of her treating Ashby as she would one of the children. Of course, Ashby gave her an annoyed look and promised to be at White's. Legally, he could spend as much money as he wanted without her approval as the law gave the husband ownership of all property, but Garrett had no doubt the duchess was wealthy in her own right.

As they left, the argument between Ashby and his wife continued. Garrett nodded to Charlotte and Arundel and was thankful to see her doing so well. He now needed to find a time to offer for her hand.

Curiosity of his father's dealings with Ashby drew him out of the comfort of his home. Nate was not happy with the plan, so Garrett sent for Arundel and Edward as he knew they would join him.

He'd been to White's before, usually with his father. As one of the most prestigious gentleman's clubs in London, his father went there for entertainment with other great minds in Parliament. Men played cards, bet far too much money, drank too much, and some participated in behavior their wives would not approve of, but would never ask about as it was too shocking for feminine ears.

Garrett asked his father, years ago, if he participated in the behavior he'd witnessed, and believed him when Cholmondeley said no. His father explained there were men in society who put on airs and claimed to be sticklers for the rules, but in private lived very differently. For a fleeting moment, he wondered if following his father and the dukes to White's was a smart venture as he might find his father was one of those men.

"How do you suggest we stay out of sight?" Edward asked as they walked into the club.

"I do not know," Garrett said with a quirk of his mouth, "It is too dark out and my eyes will not adjust. I will rely on you to keep us hidden."

Edward looked to Arundel, "I think we've found ourselves another brother. This is exactly what Charles would say. It is no wonder we are always in trouble for poor behavior with people like Charles and Haughton to guide us to these situations."

Arundel put a hand on Edward's shoulder, "Calm down. Father usually meets in a private room when he is discussing a wager."

Garrett put his hand on Arundel's shoulder and walked behind him. He only hoped they weren't too late. If the discussion was over, this entire trip would be a waste.

Slinking outside the door to a private room, Arundel confirmed their fathers were the occupants. Garrett followed as they snuck in a door leading to a serving area.

Arundel whispered, "We can listen in on the conversation through here."

If they were caught, they would look ridiculous. Sitting on the ground, all three men perked their ears toward the conversation they could hear in the main room.

"Deal the cards, Dudley," Ashby said with a grunt.

"Patience, Ashby, we are not here to play games. We are supposed to discuss the agreement we made at the beginning of summer," Dudley grumbled, clearly upset with the whole situation.

"You want out of the bet?" Ashby asked, obviously bored as he sighed.

Garrett had to admit there were sounds he never would have noticed before going blind. There was much a person could infer from sighs, inflection in tone, pauses in conversation, and many other noises made during a conversation to communicate more than words.

"I do not plan to be here late," Cholmondeley said, entering the conversation.

"You should be as concerned as I, Cholmondeley, both our children have ruined our chances. We might as well pay Ashby now and forego the humiliation of the actual loss."

"I do not plan to lose, Dudley."

"What made you agree with Haughton on this? We had a plan, Cholmondeley. Our children would marry, and we would beat Ashby at his own game."

"You do not know who you are dealing with, if you ever thought we had a chance." Cholmondeley's laughter was genuine but boastful. "Ashby's son is already married. We never had a chance to win."

Arundel looked over to Edward, "What are they talking about?"

Edward shrugged his shoulders, "Not a clue. They are speaking around the wager, but how fortunate for you our father has bet on you again."

Garrett held his hand up to quiet the twins as their fathers continued to speak.

Ashby spoke in the same bored tone he used before. "It is not my fault you cannot marry your children off."

Dudley laughed but didn't sound amused. "Yes, Ashby, you are right. Our children disappointed us by ending their engagement. But at least we do not have to worry about our sons not having the skill to bring a child into the world. You have two married sons, and neither has reproduced."

Garrett pulled both Arundel and Edward back to the ground as they fought to stand. He had no doubt they'd both charge into the room and set Dudley straight on his comment. "Both of you stop fighting me and listen," Garrett hissed.

"My sons may have failed me in producing heirs, but it is only because we agreed not to speak to them about the bet. Something you did not keep quiet, Dudley."

"I never said a word to Ruby about the gamble."

"Haughton is also unaware." It pained Garrett to hear his father speak about being a part of this gamble. He wanted to know the details so he could let his father know it was despicable.

"So, now you both have children in positions blocking them from fulfilling your side of the bet, how do you want to change the rules?"

Cholmondeley was the first to speak, "We should cut our losses and forget about the bet."

"I agree," Ashby said.

Garrett put his hands up to stop both Arundel and Edward from crying out in surprise with their father's words.

"So, I have no choice but to agree to this?" Dudley said with disgust. He sneered, loudly expressing his displeasure. "You force me to lose out on the money I could make."

"Your son has already reproduced," Ashby said. Garrett heard the sound of a coin spinning on the table. "You are the fortunate one here."

Garrett raised his eyebrows in surprise. *Is it possible Ashby craves grandchildren?*

Cholmondeley's voice broke into Garrett's thoughts, "We all agree the bet is off?"

"I must admit," Ashby said with a laugh, "I am more disappointed in the loss of this bet than I was when Arundel broke my heart and helped Norland's daughter elope with Lord Folly."

"We should leave," Arundel whispered, pulling himself off the ground. Garrett took his hand and allowed his friend to help him stand.

"Phillip," Edward said in confusion, "do you think Ashby wants grandchildren?"

"Perhaps," Arundel said with the same expression of confusion as his twin. "It is rather disturbing to think of Ashby as a grandfather."

Garrett listened to his friends' musings over children and their questions of Ashby's ability to be a loving or even caring grandfather. When they helped him back to his house, he thanked them and made his way to his chambers. There were other times he'd been disappointed in his father, but this was the worst he'd ever felt toward the man. He didn't know what possessed his father to gamble on such a sensitive topic, and would never ask, but something inside him broke and he made a vow to never make such a reprehensible wager.

Chapter 28

Charlotte ran her hands down the front of her dress. It was pretty and perfect for a musical evening. After a fortnight of receiving flowers and cards wishing her well, she was ready to reenter society completely free of any indication of the abuse she suffered at the hands of Lord Riley. As she entered the hall, she was surprised to hear Marianne speaking of the man on her mind.

"What do you think will happen now Lord Haughton is no longer engaged? He is to be at the musical tonight, isn't he?"

"Really, Marianne?" Edward said with more surprise than anything. "One would think after the gossip our family has endured we could stay out of it where others are concerned."

"I do not want to sound nosy. I just wondered what Lottie will do. She has shown interest in Lord Haughton, but Lord Branton now courts her," Marianne responded with an air of intrigue.

Everyone turned to Charlotte, which caused her more than a bit of anxiety. If she were honest with her siblings, she would tell them about her thoughts and how she'd also wondered what would happen. But since she'd last seen Haughton, there hadn't been any indication of his feelings for her. He hadn't even sent flowers as the other well-wishers had. Overall, there was much disappointment in her mind where Haughton was concerned.

"I do not know why you are all looking in my direction. Haughton may have saved my life, but he has not made an attempt to speak with me or see me in the weeks of my healing."

"Do you think his eyes will ever completely heal? I nearly burst into tears as I saw him standing on the sidelines at the last party we attended," Marianne said in a very casual way, setting Charlotte's nerves on end. Marianne was not a vicious woman, but it was obvious she thought Charlotte preferred Branton to Haughton as the casual discussion continued.

In a very careful and deliberate response, Phillip held his hand up to stop Charlotte's curt reply and spoke over her. "Haughton's accident will not be easily reversed. He came to realize this. I was happy to see him looking so well and content and if his eyes clear up completely, it will be counted as a miracle."

"I feel so sorry for Lady Ruby," Marianne continued, "so young and a broken engagement. No matter how Lord Haughton takes the blame for the arrangement not working out, it is still a stain on her reputation."

Not holding her comments in any longer, Charlotte's bitter thoughts sprang from her sharp tongue. "I also feel for Lady Ruby." The shocked look on her brothers' and sisters' faces kept her from stopping with the short statement. "When Lord Haughton finds out she was not only engaged to him, but also to Lord Madden, and had been since she found out he lost his sight in the accident, her reputation will be ruined no matter how the story is twisted. Poor little girl. Which lord of the peerage will she marry once her reputation is completely destroyed? A stain is preferable than the black hole her virtue will fall into."

She looked up to see her siblings' faces taut in shock.

Continuing her rant, she finished, "As I come to consider the situation, I do not have a single compassionate thought for Lady Ruby whatsoever."

"How did you come by this information?" Phillip asked in surprise.

"I should not have spoken. It was told to me in a confidence."

"Well, it is in the open now," Edward said with a nervous laugh.

"Please, do not tell anyone of what I spoke." Disgusted with her lack of propriety, Charlotte straightened her wrapper to leave with the group.

"I will only tell Haughton. He has a right to know," Phillip said while helping his wife with her wrapper. It was futile to argue with Phillip, and she agreed Garrett had a right to know the ending of the agreement was not his fault.

Charlotte had a lot of regret for her brash words. She remembered well the gossip and scandal surrounding Phillip and Emma the previous years. The *ton* had moved on by now, especially because they were married and there was nothing more to gossip about, but it still hurt her brother and sister-in-law.

She stayed silent on the ride to the musical. Nervous to see Lord Haughton again. She didn't care if he couldn't see clearly. She cared about his mental well-being and she didn't want him injured by the information she'd given.

As they entered the hall, she noticed Lord and Lady Cholmondeley with their daughters and younger son. She tried to remember his name, but found she'd never asked. He'd not attended the house party as he'd been at a friend's home during the summer.

"Lord Arundel," Cholmondeley said in greeting as the party approached. "Have you met my son, Lord James?"

"Yes, I have," Phillip said with a respectful bow of response.

Charlotte followed with a curtsey when she was introduced.

Phillip continued to speak. "Cholmondeley, I was told Haughton would be in attendance this evening. Is he here?"

"Yes, I am." Garrett spoke from behind them.

Charlotte turned in surprise, her heart pulsing in her ears as she looked at him. She watched her brothers as they greeted Haughton. He stood with a cane in one hand and his valet on the other ready to guide him like a companion.

Charlotte was about to speak when the evening's hostess, Lady Mayfair, appeared at Garrett's side.

"I have secured seats for you. Close to the front of the room." She spoke loudly, took Garrett's arm, and touched his face. "Poor boy, I want you to enjoy this evening even if you cannot see."

"Thank you, my lady, but it is not necessary. My sight is slowly returning, and my hearing was not injured."

She looked to the valet, her scowl indicating his presence at the party was scandalous. "You may go, I will help Lord Haughton to his seat."

Charlotte exchanged an amused glance with Emma but didn't speak out loud. Haughton must have learned to school his expressions as he didn't show any sign of annoyance. But she knew him well enough to know Lady Mayfair's actions weren't appreciated.

"Thank you for your assistance, Nate," Haughton said as Lady Mayfair held to his arm. "Lady Mayfair, I thank you for the attention you have bestowed upon me, but Nate is a valued friend and I would not have the ability to navigate society without his assistance as there are moments I do not fully see things."

"You poor boy!" Lady Mayfair shook her head and wiped tears from her eyes. "Lord Cholmondeley, please find your son a companion of his same social standing so he does not have to consort with servants."

"We will take your suggestion into consideration," Lord Cholmondeley said in an obvious attempt at humoring the hostess.

"I think I have just the person!" Lady Mayfair said with so much excitement it was difficult to stop her.

Watching Lord Haughton during the exchange made Charlotte remember the times they'd spent together, especially painting. She missed talking to him. She missed his friendship. A melancholy mood swept over her as she wondered if any man could make her as happy as Lord Haughton did that day. *Stop torturing yourself.* Those types of thoughts wouldn't do her any good. Lord Branton was a kind and generous man. She was fortunate to have him as an admirer.

"Lord Haughton!" Ruby said as she approached. Caught up in her own thoughts, Charlotte hadn't noticed Dudley and his family arrive.

"Ruby!" Lady Mayfair said with so much enthusiasm she forgot to mention who the perfect companion would be. "Oh, this is exciting!"

In Charlotte's estimation, it was revolting. *Do not be rude,* she chided.

"I usually do not have such young lovers at my musical. Every year excuses are made and engaged couples find more exciting parties to attend."

"Lady Mayfair," Haughton said with a calm expressionless face, "Ruby has chosen to end our engagement as she should not have to care for an invalid. She is far too young to have a husband who needs the amount of care I do."

Lady Mayfair patted his face and in a simpering voice she said, "Oh you have had a bit of a scuffle. You are the perfect match, and I will not hear of the engagement ending. I will not have it!" She said the last as Haughton tried to object.

"My lady," Ruby said with a pout, "Lord Haughton and I will not match. We realized this only after being separated during his recovery. I have much to say to recommend him to another, perhaps to Lady Charlotte."

Blushing as everyone looked to her, Charlotte was tongue tied and couldn't respond. Thankfully, she was saved the embarrassment by Lady Mayfair falling on her with questions of the terrible ordeal she'd suffered.

"Oh, my dear girl!" Lady Mayfair chanted as she moved from Haughton to Charlotte. "I did not even recognize you when you entered my home. I thought it would be much longer before we saw you enter society again."

This caused Charlotte to blush even more. What Ruby had been thinking, she didn't know, but Charlotte vowed to find a way to push the conversation back to the simperingly sweet, yet excruciatingly ridiculous girl. Before she could respond, Mayfair continued.

"Was it not you, Lord Haughton, who saved our sweet Charlotte from such a vicious attack? For days I have tried to imagine what would have been if Lord Haughton had not come to your aid." Lady Mayfair pulled Haughton over to force him next to Charlotte. "I need to see you side by side."

Charlotte went to move away, especially when she eyed Branton looking toward the conversation. His eyebrows quirked in curiosity and confusion.

"No. No. I will not let you hide, Lady Charlotte." Lady Mayfair causing a scene had not crossed her mind until this moment. "In truth," she said wagging her finger at Haughton, "Lady Charlotte does need a man to restore her reputation. If such a cruel act had happened to any other woman, a marriage would have occurred within hours. But, given Ashby's status in society, he stopped the cruel conversations regarding your virtue."

This was the first Charlotte had heard of her compromised situation. Putting her hands on her cheeks to cover the blush, Charlotte noticed the looks of surprise and disgust in her direction. She had not done anything to deserve censure, but suddenly received it in droves.

"Lord Haughton, now you are free from the engagement with Ruby, I will not allow you to let Charlotte's reputation suffer any longer. If I remember correctly, I heard you were holding her in your arms when help arrived." Lady Mayfair wagged her finger at him as a nanny would a naughty five-year-old caught with his hand in the pantry searching for sweets. The implications thrown her way were unsettling.

Haughton's response gave her pause, his words confirmed the terrible situation she now found herself in. "Lady Mayfair, I will not be forced into another engagement. My eyesight may not be completely clear, but I can tell when someone is manipulating a situation."

Before she could process the extent of his words, Lord Branton approached and joined the group. "Oh, Lord Branton!" Lady Mayfair exclaimed, indicating there was something to hide.

"My lady," he said acknowledging their hostess, "I could not go another moment without seeing Charlotte."

She'd given Branton permission to use her Christian name the night of the debacle with Lord Riley. He'd asked her to call him Lucas, but she didn't dare while in company with Lady Mayfair. By morning all of society would be aware of the familiarity. Discussions of engagement would occur, as it now seemed was the situation with Haughton. Charlotte wanted to acknowledge Lucas with warmth but didn't think she could while in this group.

Lady Mayfair grabbed her hands, startling her as it was an unexpected move. "I do need to warn you, Lady Charlotte, more than one person has requested you perform for us this evening."

The woman spoke as though Charlotte should find the information pleasing. She was not pleased. She was hurt and angry. The nerve of these people taking a small amount of information and making it into a scandal. How could she not have realized this would happen? How had her family kept this secret from her?

With as much grace as she could muster, Charlotte gave her hostess a smile. "I think reentering society this evening has proved far too much for me." Turning to her brother she asked, "Phillip, I am unwell, will you have the carriage brought forward? I will have it sent back for you and the others."

Thankful for her brother's understanding, he nodded his head. "I think Lady Arundel and I are also done for the evening. We will accompany you home."

"Oh, my dear girl!" Lady Mayfair simpered with Charlotte's pronouncement. "You do look rather pale." In a more panicked tone she continued, "Oh, my dear! I have smelling salts nearby in case you need them."

"That will not be necessary, but I thank you all the same."

Not listening to Charlotte's statement, Lady Mayfair turned to a maid who stood close by. "Penny, fetch the smelling salts. I think she is going to swoon."

Charlotte had never swooned, and the insinuation stung as sharply as the assumptions of her virtue. It was true she recently faked the action, but she had never involuntarily lost consciousness as other women and was not about to allow her hostess to make her look the fool, although swooning might be preferable to watching the ridiculous woman overreact to the discomfort of a guest.

Smelling salts were thrust under her nose, the stench forcing Charlotte to step back and hit into a gentleman standing behind her. Haughton grabbed her arm in an effort to steady her and keep her from falling, but he did not succeed. It was an unfortunate chain reaction she could not have foreseen. She and Haughton both fell into the man, causing him to lose hold of the glass in his hand, which happened to be filled with a brown liquid. The contents split out on his companion's very white dress bringing a screech into the air and a stop to all discussions.

Somehow during the entire debacle, Charlotte landed on top of Lord Haughton. Mortified by the current situation she found herself in, Charlotte allowed her body to lie limp as for the second time in her life she faked a swoon. *I have really got to find a better solution to these scandalous situations I find myself in,* she thought as Lady Mayfair and her brothers jumped into action.

Calls for a physician were sent out by people around them, and Charlotte thought about waking, but didn't. When she realized Haughton was unconscious it made her feel even worse for pretending.

It took everything she had to stay limp, yet she'd done it before and knew success would be had by staying calm and not reacting until another smelling salt was thrust under her nose. She was thankful to be awake when word came that with this last bump to Haughton's head his sight was fully restored.

Chapter 29

Releasing Haughton from their engagement gave Ruby the ability to fully accept Madden's proposal. Excited over the prospect of being with the man she loved, she wrote a letter to Madden and asked him to attend the musical.

While Lady Mayfair simpered over Lord Haughton and Lady Charlotte, Ruby caught Madden's eye. In an attempt to move closer to him, she looked around and found her escape, only to have her father take hold of her arm.

Pulling her close enough so he could whisper, her father repeated the orders from earlier in the day. "You have a choice between Lord Farland and Duke Chasworth."

"You do not need to remind me of your edict." She exchanged a look with her mother. After the duke laid down the orders for finding another wealthy man to marry her, she confided in her mother about Lord Madden's proposal. Surprisingly, her mother supported her decision.

She'd packed a bag and hid it in the boot on the carriage. When her father's head was turned, she'd slip out of the musical and leave with Madden for Gretna Green. Her mother promised she'd always be welcome at their home, but Ruby planned to stay away until her father recovered from the betrayal.

When Lady Charlotte and Lord Haughton fell into Mr. Wells and the crowd gathered around them, Ruby and Madden slipped out to the patio.

"Are you certain you want to run away? We could marry here. I will buy a special license and we can be married by tomorrow."

"My father will stop any wedding here in London. If we leave now, he will be busy in the game room and not notice I have left."

Madden looked back to the party. Ruby followed his gaze and made a mental note to send a thank you card to Charlotte and Haughton. The scandal Haughton and Charlotte were currently creating was enough to keep everyone busy for an escape out of the city.

"We should have left from Wentworth Hall. The trip would have been shorter." Madden's unromantic thought made her sigh.

Ruby took hold of his hand and squeezed it as he helped her retrieve her bag. He assisted her into his carriage, and a wave of happiness hit her as he instructed his driver to take them to Gretna Green.

"Should we take side roads?" Ruby worried her father would find them. Gretna Green would take longer to reach than they had that night.

"We will be successful, my love. Do not fear discovery."

Her hands shook as she sat next to the man she would marry. There were so many reasons why she loved Madden. But in that moment, as the carriage raced out of London, she wondered if this was the right course of action. He'd offered to marry her in a respectable manner. The regretful part of her wondered if it would have been better to do as he said and get a special license.

Am I making the right decision?

She looked at his lips as he spoke. If he kissed her at that moment, it would calm her fears and stop the questions. But he didn't kiss her.

"What do you think your father will do when he discovers you are gone?"

"I think we should talk about something else." She put her hands under her legs to try and calm the nervous jitters. "I love you."

Madden's face, hidden in the shadows of the dark carriage, wasn't visible to her. She wished they were escaping the city during the day. He'd told her he loved her while they were at the house party, so she didn't need the words. She needed to see his love for her.

As though he read her mind, Madden leaned forward and kissed Ruby. As the carriage bumped along through the countryside, Ruby's fears melted away. This was the right decision. Nothing had ever felt so right.

Chapter 30

"Lady Charlotte," Lucas said as she entered the room. In truth, she'd been waiting for a visit from him. Since the musical, she'd kept to Lancaster house and avoided all invitations. She noticed the use of her title, and cringed.

"Lord Branton," she said with a curtsey.

"Are you still unwell?"

"I have recovered."

"I must admit I was surprised you have not attended any gatherings since the musical." Lucas was nervous. She should not think of him as Lucas anymore as he set the tone of their discussion.

"Although I am well, I cannot abide the gossip surrounding Lord Haughton and I." As she said the words, she noticed his sigh and nod. He knew exactly what she was speaking of. It was obvious by the sympathetic look she received.

"This is the reason I am here today." Sitting and motioning to the sofa, Charlotte waited for him to gather the words he wished to say. "Lottie," she smiled as he spoke informally, "I admire and respect you. You are a beautiful and strong woman. If not for Haughton, I would ask you to be my wife and put an end to the gossip surrounding you. But I respect him and know he cares for you."

She cut him off. "How do you know he cares for me?"

Branton shook his head and laughed before giving into her insecurity. "I see it in the way he looks at you. Now he has his sight back, I dread the moment you and he attend the same gathering."

When he paused for breath, she asked, "Are you ending our courtship?"

"Yes. I will never compare to Haughton in your eyes. I need to find a woman who considers me to be the one who lights up the night sky."

These words caused her heart to ache. Lucas Grantham, the Earl of Branton was one of the kindest men she knew. Although she didn't love him, she knew if they had married, he would have been a generous husband and she would have grown to love him.

When she didn't speak, he stood to leave. As he neared the door to the parlor, Charlotte called out. "Lucas," her voice broke. Holding back the tears she asked, "Will you still be my friend?"

"Yes," he said crossing the room back to her. "I will consider it an honor to have you as one of my dearest friends." Kissing her hand in farewell, Lucas left her standing with tears in her eyes. He left without looking back.

She cared about his feelings and there was a sincere regret for the relationship not working. Charlotte sat on the sofa and cried for the pain she'd seen in his eyes knowing she was the cause of it.

"My lady?" Charlotte looked up at the sound of Collin's voice.

Will this morning never end? "Collin, I do not care to discuss anything with you. I have asked you to leave me alone." Her words could be taken as rude, but this man was far too persistent for his own good. She would need to find a way to have her father send him to a different property.

"You were just snubbed by a lord of the peerage, and you still consider me beneath you? If you knew what all of London is saying, you would not be so high handed." Collin's words caused her to pause. His smug tone was not lost on her. But she focused on the gossip.

"How do you know what is said about me?" It was obvious people were gossiping. She'd expected it. But to know the servants were listening to rumors about her was unnerving. Drying the tears she spilt for Lucas, Charlotte glared at Collin. "Tell me what they are saying."

"Poor little rich girl!" Collin mocked. Laughing at her indignation, he continued, "A ruined woman still believes she is too good for a lowly footman. You will do no better than me now all of London considers you to be a wanton."

A wanton! She knew her reputation currently suffered, but it wasn't anything so terrible her father wouldn't be able to stop the gossip. Ashby was respected and her family name should be enough to restore her reputation. She did admit, but only inwardly, it had been a poor choice to fake a swoon for the second time. She lay on Haughton far too long for it to be considered an accident. Although, in her opinion the blame did lay at Lady Mayfair's feet. If not for the meddlesome woman, Charlotte wouldn't have had to fake a swoon.

Realizing Collin still spoke, Charlotte stopped thinking about the assumptions he was making and moved to leave him in the parlor. She looked to the door and saw her father standing in stunned silence. *How much had he heard?* The disgust on his face told her she was no longer his little girl.

"Get out of my house!" Ashby yelled.

Charlotte looked away and moved to leave the room. If her father wanted her out, she would go. Without a plan, she worried for her future, but prayed Phillip would take her in. His home, Arundel Keep, was a haven from Ashby. Perhaps he'd let it be hers as well.

Before she walked past him, she said, "I am sorry to disappoint you, Father."

Ashby growled, "Not you. I want him out of my house." Relief with the understanding of his words, Charlotte allowed her father to embrace her. "How could you think I was speaking to you?" It was true, Ashby was a vicious man, when it came to Phillip, gambling, and now sometimes Edward, but he'd always been more caring toward Charlotte and Marianne. They were his daughters.

"My reputation is ruined. Lord Branton ended our courtship this morning." There was so much more she could have said, but she didn't as her words were swallowed up in a giant sob of heartache.

"Your reputation is fine. Lord Haughton will propose marriage before the week is out, and if he does not do it of his own choice, I will make certain it happens within a fortnight. I will not have the same type of scandal we had with Lord and Lady Arundel."

Relieved by his words, Charlotte was not about to remind her father he was a big reason that scandal took place. He was a tolerant man, until reminded of his indiscretions. In Ashby's estimation, dukes were always right.

Chapter 31

When Garret entered the party, he knew the broken engagement, Ruby and Madden's elopement, and the debacle with Charlotte had been center of conversation. Since falling to the ground with Charlotte, and hitting his head again, his eyesight had improved completely. Although it hadn't been shouted from the castle walls, it spread through society like a juicy piece of gossip.

His recovery was a source of entertainment for dinner parties and social settings. A broken engagement and now the situation with Charlotte swooning at the musical, he had become infamous and, from the whispers he heard, a rake.

Even with this newfound reputation, Garrett was shocked to find the number of women gathering to speak with him. If their fathers weren't off playing cards, he was certain not a single woman would be vying for his attentions.

Teeth clenched and clinging to his mother's arm, he said, "Do not leave me. I should have stayed home."

His mother turned with an indulgent look. Chiding him, she patted his arm. "Or you should have offered for Lady Charlotte. Too many women are looking for a man who will save them as you have done for her."

"Or they are in search of a title and wealth, and now I am no longer blind, they have taken me off a shelf."

His mother laughed at him, "You were never on a shelf, Garrett."

I should have stayed home, he said to himself as he escorted his mother through the crowds of women. "I will be your partner in whist."

His mother patted his hand. "You will not! I want to win, and you are far too distracted."

He walked her to a chair so she could enjoy the evening with conversation and card games. It was strange how people simply didn't care if he heard what they said, others tried to hide their conversations, but being blind didn't make him deaf as some of them thought and now his sight was returned, he had the learned sense of a blind man to include in his repertoire of— did he have a gossip repertoire?

"Lord Haughton," Miss Whitby said in a startlingly loud voice, making her the center of entertainment.

"Miss Whitby." He'd been introduced to her only once before, and it had been the previous season at a party similar to this one. She was a sly woman, and he did not know how to respond to her statements.

She gave a nervous laugh, "I did not think you would recognize me."

"I am no longer blind, as my eyes have healed." He tried not to sound rude, but it was rather difficult. He had walked away from his mother on his own and he no longer carried a cane. Simple deductive tactics could have been used to determine this information on her part.

"Oh!" She batted her eyes at him and played the normal games of a debutant, which might have worked before he fell for the very beautiful and intelligent Lady Charlotte. She'd admitted to him only weeks before of her deceit in swooning while at Wentworth Hall. He knew this last swoon was much the same, at least he expected it was. If he told anyone this information though, he'd be considered a cad. Inwardly deciding it was not a terrible addition, he decided he could add it to the list of titles following his name. Garrett Calder the Earl of Haughton, a rake and a cad. It all sounded so nice when together.

He looked to Miss Whitby as she'd said something he missed. The batting of eyes and pouting of her lips were all in vain. His love for Charlotte trumped the ridiculous games these women would play to gain a man's affections.

"Will you be my whist partner?" Miss Whitby asked, placing her gloved hand on his arm.

"I have never done well at card games. My own mother chose her friend as a partner instead of me."

"Oh, you must be teasing Lord Haughton," Miss Whitby called out flirtatiously, hitting his arm with an annoying giggle.

"There is no need to flatter me." He was tired of insincere people and this game they played in society was wearing on his soul.

She squeezed his arm and batted her eyes, "Will you walk with me?"

Unable to stand the conversation, he shook his head. He didn't care to be caught in a quiet corner or secret assignation with this woman. Not caring if he sounded rude, he said, "No, I prefer to stay where I am." Surely a man who'd survived nearly dying in a fire, falling from a horse, and blindness could forego the torture of women throwing themselves at him.

She giggled, "You are such a tease, my lord. A girl might get the impression you were flirting with her."

He was not about to be stuck in another engagement due to a misunderstanding or an over excited female. When he became engaged again, it would be with the woman he loved. "Miss Whitby, I apologize for any misunderstanding between us, but I am not teasing you. I am tired, bored, and in a foul mood. I would prefer to be home. Please go back to your group of friends and report your attempt at winning my fortune, so I may spend my evening in peace."

It was harsh, but he was tired of the constant gossip and chatter about his situation. As he saw her gaping mouth turn up in a smile, the guilt from his comments washed away. He needed a plan for regaining composure and temperament.

He walked away without another word in her direction and found a chair at a game of cards. Knowing his luck always went sour, he didn't place any bets he would regret losing. It annoyed him Charlotte wasn't in attendance. Ashby and his family always attended the card night at Lord and Lady Cadishs' home. What made them stay away? He stayed in his chair for another hour before sending a servant to fetch his parents, claiming a headache. London as a whole was tiresome. The constant gossip, balls, insincere comments, and more bothered him. He'd never enjoyed being in London and sitting at this house party reminded him of his dislike for the activity.

The carriage ride home was full of Lillian and Hazel discussing their conquests of the evening. He laid his head back and closed his eyes, thinking of the country, riding Sun Dancer in the open meadows around Cheshire, and the quiet evenings when Hazel's words pierced his thoughts.

"Lady Charlotte and Lady Ruby were the topics of conversation in every group this evening. It is terrible the things people are saying about them."

"Hazel, your brother has a headache. Leave him in peace." His mother's soft chide wasn't stern.

Hazel kept silent for only a second or two before continuing. "Garrett, can you believe they think you will not ask for her hand?"

There was no need to open his eyes as he knew everyone in the carriage was looking at him.

"It is no one's business if I do or do not propose." Garrett spoke to the family as a whole. He'd been stuck in an engagement with Ruby for far too long. Was it too much to ask for time to breathe before entering another?

His father cleared his throat. Garrett opened his eyes to give him respect. "Ashby sent a letter this morning. He is expecting you to restore Lady Charlotte's reputation."

He hadn't confronted his father about the meeting he eavesdropped on while at White's. At first it was because he didn't know what to say and then his sight clearing up was an excuse to ignore the nagging curiosity. But now he needed to know if there were any ulterior motives for his father's encouragement toward entering an engagement.

"I am not certain she needs saving, Father. Ashby and Arundel are well known among the peerage. Charlotte will not suffer long."

Garrett didn't expect his mother's outburst. "I raised you better than this! A woman needs your saving, and you would put your needs above hers?"

"It is not about my needs, Mother." He took a deep breath. "I simply want to know what Father will get out of the connection."

Cholmondeley's eyebrows raised as the light from the moon shone through the carriage window. "What are you implying?"

Gaining courage from the shocked look on his father's face, he continued. "I want to know the terms of the gamble you have with Dudley and Ashby."

"How did you come by this information?" Cholmondeley asked, surprise clearly written on his face. He didn't give any explanations and then shame filled his eyes as he looked down at the ground.

"I knew something had to be wrong when you did not take action to help me out of the situation with Ruby. I begged for help and after the accident you still did not help as I asked." Continuing to speak would have only brought out more whining, so he waited for Cholmondeley to respond.

"I was caught in between two men more powerful than I, and Dudley made some poor investments." Cholmondeley had never looked so small and pathetic. He was a marquess and shouldn't look so downtrodden. "I did not have the ability to help you out of the situation with Lady Ruby. But I promise you, Ashby and Dudley have agreed to end the bet."

"What happens if I ask for Charlotte's hand? What bet will come from it?"

"There will not be another wager, Garrett. I promise you."

"Then why does Ashby expect a proposal?"

"You are too well versed in society and the expectations of your station to ask such a question."

His mother reached forward and touched his hand. "I thought you were not adverse to Lady Charlotte."

Garrett sighed, "I am more than happy to offer for Charlotte's hand, but I will not be forced into another engagement. This needs to be a decision I make with Charlotte."

Lillian, in a loud whisper so everyone could hear, made Garrett realize his stubborn pride had been ridiculous. "How is Charlotte supposed to be part of the decision if you do not speak with her or even court her?"

This was a legitimate question, and he had no answer for his sister other than to nod in her direction to show the message was received. Without anything left to say, Garrett exited the carriage when he was able and left for his chambers. He wanted to be alone.

"My lord," Nate said, interrupting Garrett's thoughts, "it is time to dress for the dinner party at Lancaster House."

Spending the previous night and now day in his room to consider how he would handle the situation with Charlotte, Garrett looked toward his valet and squinted his eyes in confusion. "I did not know about a dinner invitation. When did it arrive?"

"Is it not typical for these types of soirée to be planned at least a week in advance?"

"Yes, I do apologize for my ridiculous question. I just want to know why I was not informed of the invite."

"I do not know, my lord." Nate's voice sounded annoyed. Since he'd become companion to a blind man, then no longer needed in the capacity, Nate had been unsatisfied.

"Thank you for informing me."

"Do you have a preference on what you will wear?"

While blind, he'd allowed Nate to choose his clothing. It was oddly normal to give a preference to him now. "Whatever you think will look best for this gathering will be fine."

Nate looked pleased by his acquiescing, which in turn made dressing less stressful. He thought about discussing the attitude with Nate but decided it would be best to see if things calmed down and over time became what they once were.

"Very good, my lord. I thought the blue would look nice."

"Fine. Nate, do you know what the purpose of this dinner invitation is?" He hadn't expected to meet with Charlotte or anyone in Ashby's family for at least another day or so. His plan was to invite Charlotte for a ride through Hyde Park. Discuss their situation and what she wanted from their scandal.

"The invitation did not say, my lord. Although if you do not mind a bit of speculation and rumor with my answer."

Garrett smiled and nodded. This was the old Nate. The one before his accident and added responsibilities. "Tell me what you have heard."

"I heard Duke Ashby is announcing the upcoming marriage of one of his children."

"Who?"

"Well, I am not sure if it is a daughter or the youngest son."

"Where did you hear this rumor? I did not know any of his children were attached."

"There is much speculation it is an attachment between you and Lady Charlotte. But I told everyone I would know if my master were to be married."

Without allowing Nate to tie his cravat, Garrett rushed from the room toward his father's chambers. He knocked three times before his father's valet opened the door. Cholmondeley stood in a pristine black ensemble.

"What is the purpose of this soirée at Lancaster House?"

Raising his eyebrows in confusion, Cholmondeley broke into a laugh. "Are you concerned?"

"Yes. The rumors surround Charlotte and I."

Seeing his father's reaction told him he'd behaved terribly. The accusation he thrust toward the man was unwarranted, but to his relief Cholmondeley took it in stride.

"Oh, Garrett," he said, waving his valet over to help him straighten out his clothing. "When did you start listening to gossip and taking it so seriously?"

Had he spent too much time in his chambers thinking about the scandal to realize this was simply another gathering of society? There did not need to be an exact reason other than it was the London Season and Duke and Duchess Ashby always held a soirée. Feeling more than a bit ridiculous, Garrett backed toward the door.

"I must admit, Haughton, you were never so paranoid before this season. Does London bother you so much you cannot enjoy a party?"

His father was correct. He hated London for all of the games women and their mothers played on the affections of men, and he hated the societal expectations thrust upon him merely due to his station in life. He was fortunate to have been born to a marquess and marchioness and considered it was only fate that had not landed him as the child of a stable master, cook, maid, footman, or chimney sweep. He very well could be starving on the streets as an orphan shining shoes, but for some reason God placed him in a wealthy and loving family.

Feeling more than a little foolish, he apologized and left his father to finish dressing. Perhaps this wasn't Ashby's plan to get him in the house and make him offer for his daughter. And then there was the question of why he was fighting this engagement so much. He still hadn't figured that answer out. He was taken by Charlotte's love for painting, her beauty, her lovely and cheerful personality, the way she looked when her cheeks filled with a blush, and he could list out many other qualities she possessed.

She would make a wonderful wife and mother, so why did he hesitate? She was not forcing him into an engagement as Ruby had. When he kissed Charlotte, she faked a swoon so they wouldn't be caught in a scandal. Which made him remember he needed to find out about this last swoon. Real or fake? He had to know and would not rest until—

"My lord, do you want to have your cravat tied? Or will you go to the gathering with it in the current state of disarray?"

Looking down at his partially dressed self, he nodded and crossed back to his room. His mind was so full of Charlotte he did not know if he would ever rid her from his thoughts, but did he want her gone? She was a ray of sunlight and hope to him. He would speak with her this evening and arrange a ride through Hyde Park to discuss their future. With this plan, he felt lighter than he had for many months. This was the perfect solution to his worries and concerns.

He finished dressing and made his way to the carriage which would take them to Lancaster House. It was a short ride, and would have been faster on foot, but his parents insisted on arriving in a carriage.

Upon entering, he searched the ballroom for Charlotte. Lancaster House was everything he expected. Large, expensive, and gaudy. Spotting her across the room, Garrett decided he would ask for her hand that night. Before he could cross the room, however, he heard raised voices making him turn back to the entryway. Riley and Ashby stood in heated discussion.

"Riley, we can discuss your needs tomorrow. Right now, I am entertaining *invited* guests." If Ashby had ever spoken to Garrett in such a tone or with the disgusted glare on his face, Garrett would have run for hiding. Ashby held the collective breath of the room with his anger emanating from his piercing eyes, which somehow looked black in the lighting.

"No Ashby, I will not be the one shunned from society," Riley yelled. "If you had taken care not to invite Cholmondeley's family to the house party this summer, I would have fulfilled my end of our bargain and I would have won the bet."

Another bet? Ashby was fortunate all of society envied his wealth and power, otherwise he might be ousted from the country with the antics he played.

"I would have won Charlotte's hand if that mongrel had not been there to pull her attentions away from me."

Mongrel? Garrett questioned as he looked up to find Riley walking toward him. He didn't have time to defend himself and found Riley's hands closed around his neck. Thankfully his father, Arundel, and Edward extricated Riley from Garrett's body and neck before any harm could come to him, but it was unnerving to think what could have happened.

"You owe me, Haughton. You owe me the money I lost to Ashby!" Riley yelled as he was pulled from the room.

Although the soirée had started only a short time previous, it came to a quick close with guests leaving in droves. Garrett wondered to himself if this would be the end of Ashby, and then looked over at the man to see how many of his admirers were complementing Ashby on handling the situation with grace and poise. Ashby would never learn.

"Are you all right?" Garrett turned to see Charlotte standing next to him. She was everything he remembered from when he'd had perfect sight. Not having seen her since the blurriness left, he'd hadn't the chance to admire her properly.

"Yes." This was all he could say as he stared into her deep ocean blue eyes. Remembering there had been a plan to speak with her, he asked, "Will you ride with me in Hyde Park tomorrow?"

Charlotte laughed, "Are you certain you want to be seen in public with me? It might cause further scandal and certainly conjecture where we are concerned."

In a very brazen move, Garrett decided scandal with Charlotte wasn't that bad. Ashby had caused more than enough problems for the evening, he might as well add to the mix. He pulled Charlotte into his arms and kissed her.

The gasps of surprise from people in the room did not stop him. The clearing of throats from more than one man only increased his desire to kiss the soft tender lips of the woman he held in his arms.

"Garrett!" His mother's censure brought the passion to a halt. As he pulled away, he looked Charlotte in the eyes and whispered, "If you were going to fake a swoon, you should have already done so."

"I enjoyed it too much to swoon, my lord."

"We will have to marry now," he said looking into her sparkling eyes.

Charlotte nodded with a disappointed frown. He nearly asked what the problem was, when she pulled at his cravat and went up on her toes to continue their kiss.

Chapter 32

Charlotte was overwhelmingly happy she'd approached Haughton when she did. A kiss was the last thing she'd expected, but knowing he loved her boosted her confidence. As Ashby stopped the scene they made in front of the stunned guests, Charlotte felt the familiar creep of a blush raising in her face.

"Lord Haughton, do you have something you need to say to me?" Ashby growled.

Charlotte closed her eyes in fear. Would Haughton realize he'd be stuck with Ashby as a father by marrying her? Would he leave once the realization of who he was tying himself to would overwhelm the feelings he had for her? Was the love she saw in his large chocolate eyes only moments before be easily swayed by connections?

"Yes, Duke, I apologize for not speaking to you earlier."

"You have a duty to me as her father, before offering to my daughter. Did Cholmondeley not teach you etiquette?"

"Father," Charlotte tried to calm him as she could see his temper rising. It would not be good for anyone if Ashby lost control.

"We will take this to my study," Ashby said, turning from Haughton.

Charlotte tried to hide the smile on her face as she looked back to Haughton. Biting her lips, she nodded her head to let him know they should follow. When they reached the study, she noticed her mother, Phillip, and Haughton's parents followed them in.

"Haughton, normally I would not condone a man speaking to one of my daughters about marriage without consulting me first but given the constant scandal you bring to our families each time you are together, I will forgive your indiscretion.

Charlotte wanted to bury her head in her mother's shoulder in shame. Her father called it an indiscretion! She could not deny the accusation of scandal she and Haughton were a part of, as they did seem to cause a lot of gossip of late.

"I assure you I meant no disrespect. I thought it would be right to discuss the option with Charlotte to see if she was agreeable before moving forward with speaking to you."

"What does it matter if she is agreeable? Marriage is an arrangement between the father and the suitor."

"I apologize, your grace."

Charlotte looked to her mother for help. Ashby could be very stalwart and stuck to tradition at times.

Always thankful for her oldest brother, Phillip interrupted the conversation. "Father, you know there are some of us in society who prefer a love match over the haggling of dowry and indifference."

"Arundel, there are not many people like you and your wife. It is only by our long standing in society and ability to host lavish parties that we were able to reduce the scandal of your marriage. Charlotte and the rest of my children know a love match would be disastrous to our situation. We are still on precarious grounds."

Charlotte forced the smile on her face to go away as she realized her father did not know Edward loved Anne before they were married. She had a feeling all of her siblings would marry for love. They'd be an infamous and extremely scandalous group among the *ton*. The thought of it brought a smile back to her face.

Knowing her words would injure her father, she could not let Lord Haughton believe she was indifferent to him. "Father, you will have to find a way to reduce the scandal once again, because I am in love with Lord Haughton and I am accepting his proposal."

Her father grumbled something she didn't care to hear as she crossed the room and stood in front of Haughton. "I am in love with you. When you are near, I usually forget to breathe."

"I am in love with you as well," Haughton replied, "but, I will respect your father and continue discussions with him."

Charlotte smiled and nodded, "Please remember you are marrying me and not him. We do not have to live anywhere near Wentworth Hall."

"Do not fear, my love. I will not change my mind no matter what Ashby says."

"I would suggest you remember this as you speak with him. He can be cunning at times."

"Charlotte, leave with your mother and Lady Cholmondeley. We men have much to discuss," Ashby said with the air of one who was ready to make a deal. This was her father in his best form. He would make a show of the dowry discussions.

Before leaving her fiancé, she looked into his eyes, "Do not show fear and doubt, and do not be humble. He will take advantage of you."

Garrett winked at her. "I promise I will take him for everything I can."

With this talisman in her heart, she gracefully left the room to discuss her trousseau and wedding plans.

Chapter 33

Duke Ashby scoffed at the requested amount. Cholmondeley locked eyes with the duke. Garrett sat in his overstuffed chair next to Arundel waiting for the outburst.

Leaning forward on his desk, Ashby growled. "Are you attempting to rob me?"

"Not in the least. A marriage to my son will restore Lady Charlotte's reputation. He has other choices." Cholmondeley smirked as they all watched Ashby's face go deep red.

"Father, you forget I took part in the scandals." Garrett hoped to start the marriage off with common ground, instead of having the powerful duke as an enemy.

"Quiet, Haughton. You and Arundel are to watch and learn how to negotiate a marriage contract." Cholmondeley turned so the duke couldn't see his smile. Garrett realized his father was enjoying the argument.

"I already know how to negotiate one. Do you forget I am married?" Arundel wasn't amused with their fathers.

"And you received a pittance for her. But what would you expect for a barren woman?" Ashby glowered at his son.

"Emma is not barren."

"She has yet to produce an heir or even a female child."

Sighing, Arundel shook his head. "We are here to discuss Charlotte's dowry. Please continue your argument."

"Haughton!" Ashby yelled Garrett's title while keeping eye contact with the marquess. "How soon do you plan to produce an heir?"

"What does this have to do with the conversation?" Cholmondeley moved from his seat to stand behind Garrett's chair. "Such things are out of Garrett's control."

"Fine, Cholmondeley. I agree. Reproduction is out of our hands. I will agree to fifty thousand pounds upon the marriage, and an additional twenty thousand when they bring a child into the marriage."

Cholmondeley walked back to his chair and sat. Looking as though he gave the offer serious consideration, he suddenly slammed his fist on the arm of the chair. "I told you a hundred thousand pounds for the marriage and a home with land."

"I have other children who require an inheritance."

"This request will not empty your coffers."

Tired of the negotiations, Garrett stood and left the room without notice of the duke and marquess. He smiled when he saw Charlotte standing in the hall.

"Are you bored with the negotiations already?" Charlotte asked, walking into his outstretched arms.

"When I return, they will still be haggling over the same amounts. When we have daughters ready for marriage, I will give their suitors whatever cost they ask, just to avoid a situation as this."

"You will not!" Charlotte playfully punched his arm. "I imagine you will haggle as your father is right now."

"I wish we were already married."

"As do I. Although, this is your fault."

"What do you mean by that?"

"If you had not delayed in asking for my hand, negotiations would be finished, and we would be on our wedding tour."

"I fear no matter when negotiations started, we would still be in a freeze as neither of our fathers can agree to an amount."

"Is there anything we can do to encourage them along?" Charlotte's pleading eyes melted his heart. "If they never come to an agreement, we will never be wed."

Pulling her into an embrace, he gave a low chuckle. "I will get a special license for us, and we will not have to worry about either of our fathers being in attendance."

"What if they never come to an agreement and my father blocks the special license?"

"We will follow Ruby and Madden to Gretna Green. An increase in the scandal will make us the most infamous couple the *ton* has produced in all of history." He spoke in jest, then stiffened as Ashby shouted over their conversation.

"None of my children will marry in Gretna Green. Can you imagine the scandal?" Asbhy's grumbling continued. "Fine, Cholmondeley, a dowry of one hundred thousand pounds and the property in Scotland."

"Does this mean we can marry next week?" Charlotte asked. The excitement in her voice brought him joy.

"Tell your mother we'll be leaving for Cheshire in the morning," Ashby called out.

Knowing the duke and his own father were so close by and could not only hear their conversation but see into the hall, Garrett did not kiss his betrothed. He waited for her to walk away before he went back into the den of haughty men to finish the discussion and sign the dowry agreement.

Chapter 34

Charlotte imagined her wedding day filled with family, which is exactly what her mother and Lady Cholmondeley planned. Giddy with excitement, Charlotte imagined standing in front of her family with Haughton.

"Where are you?" Marianne asked, smiling at her as though she expected a romantic answer.

Marianne, Emma, and Anne helped her dress and her maid did her hair. She now stood in the parlor looking in a floor length mirror brought in for the purpose of preparing for her wedding. "I wonder what it will feel like to be called by the name Lady Haughton."

As she said the words, she realized the thought hadn't crossed her mind until that moment. It was a happy thought. She looked around the large room and realized this would be her home going forward. She and Haughton were to inherit Sky Manor in Scotland and planned to spend part of the year there, but this would be their main home.

She would be the Countess of Haughton within the hour, and one day she would be the Marchioness of Cholmondeley. And it was a union of love. She'd never imagined marrying for love until her brothers found Emma and Anne.

Charlotte smiled as her father came to retrieve her. "Are you ready?"

"Nervous." Charlotte's squeak put smiles on everyone's faces, even her own. "May I have a moment alone to collect myself?"

"Yes, we will wait for you in the hall." Ashby patted her hand. "Do not keep him waiting. He has robbed me of my daughter and my fortune."

"I only need a minute."

As everyone left, Charlotte put her shaking hand over her heart. "Why am I so nervous?" She asked the question while looking in the mirror. Trying out the title, she again spoke out loud and to herself. "Lady Haughton. Good day, my name is Lady Haughton."

A thrill of excitement followed each pronouncement. But as her heart continued to pound, she realized she needed fresh air. Walking to the doors leading out to the patio, Charlotte opened them to feel the cool winter breeze.

"Good morning, Lottie."

Turning at the familiar voice, Charlotte hoped she was wrong. The man standing before her fit the tight pinched voice she remembered as Collin.

"What are you doing here?" Getting married at Cholmondeley Hall meant only the family members and friends invited would be in attendance. Collin didn't fit that description.

Charlotte should have called out the minute she'd seen Collin, but the shock of his arrival left her speechless. Turning to go back in the house, Charlotte wanted nothing more than to be married to Lord Haughton. She was no longer nervous of becoming a countess.

"I only wanted to speak with you. Please do not leave." Collin's plea brought out her compassion. "I wanted to apologize."

Turning back, she wanted to convey the message of *you are forgiven* and *go away*. "Say what you need, then leave."

"Please walk with me?"

"I am to be married. Everyone is waiting on me." She turned to go back in the parlor when Collin took hold of her arm. Yanking it away, Charlotte glared at the footman.

"I came to speak with you. Will you not give me a moment of your time?"

"No. It is not wise. I forgive you and pray you find joy and peace."

Charlotte again turned to go back in the house when Collin pulled her into his arms. The scream she let out was muffled by his hand. Charlotte fought, trying to get away. She kicked his leg, causing him to stumble and fall backwards pulling her down with him.

Rolling away from his grasp, Charlotte screamed, with fear, for anyone in hearing to help. Within seconds her father and brothers were running out the doors, Lord Haughton with them. Her eyes full of tears caused the scene before her to blur. As Haughton lifted her from the ground, she wrapped her arms around his neck and experienced the familiar rush of love as he carried her back inside.

It took time for her to realize she was safe. Holding tight to Haughton, Charlotte cried until her heart no longer raced. There had been a moment she'd feared everything she had, Lord Haughton, a future marriage, her family, everything she loved would be taken from her.

"We should delay the wedding." Ashby spoke in a hushed whisper, but his voice pierced her thoughts and sent her back into worry. If they delayed, what would happen next?

"No. I only need a moment." She wiped the tears with a handkerchief she hadn't realized she held.

"Charlotte, we will delay a week at most." Her mother's words were meant to calm her, instead they caused renewed panic.

"A week? Why so long?" Turning to the crowd around them, Charlotte wasn't happy to see the room full. Her scream brought both her and Haughton's family to the room.

"Your dress is torn. You will need a new one." Her mother lifted the dirt-stained fabric.

Renewed tears at the state of her dress and the impossibility of the wedding, Charlotte buried her head in Haughton's shoulder. She could wear any dress to be married in, it didn't have to be new. But this one she chose because it made her feel pretty.

Her father cleared his throat. "It is inappropriate for you to continue holding my daughter, Haughton. We will take her to her chambers now."

"You are right, Ashby. I would use the word scandalous to define this." Haughton's words brought her head up.

"What do you mean?" Her voice trembled with the thought of further ruin.

"I do not think a week will be appropriate for the level of scandal we are now creating. I will marry you this very moment, ripped dress, tear-stained eyes, scandal and all."

When he first started talking, she wasn't sure her heart could take anymore. The loving way he gazed upon her let her know the dress didn't matter. She nodded and dried the renewal of tears, this time brought on by a heart filled with love.

"If the wedding is to proceed, you should wear something clean." Her mother's arm came around her to guide her away.

"Your hair also needs to be fixed." Lady Cholmondeley rushed forward to help. "We will be but another moment. You may all go back to the drawing room to wait."

Charlotte had one last look at Haughton as she was whisked away to redress for the wedding. This time, when she was ready, instead of fear for the unknown future, she knew Haughton was the soul mate she'd hoped to find. Butterflies joyfully danced in her stomach as she took her father's arm and allowed him to lead her to the drawing room. Seeing Garrett smile at her, a smile of genuine pleasure, calmed her nerves. This was the man who loved her. He'd proved his love over and over throughout the past months. Charlotte stood next to Haughton, holding his hands in anticipation of the vicar's final words pronouncing them man and wife.

She listened to the admonitions guiding them to a marriage of communication. It was obvious the vicar had not been informed of their mutual feelings of love. A deed of her father, she guessed, as a way to hide or delay the scandal of allowing them to marry for love. She smiled and experienced the pure joy of seeing Garrett return her smile.

The vicar paused, which caused Charlotte to look up at him. "I usually do not see couples of your station in love during the ceremony."

The pronouncement of Lord and Lady Haughton brought her more joy than she originally anticipated. Breaking tradition, Haughton pulled her into an embrace and placed a very tender, very passionate, very welcome kiss on her lips. Charlotte momentarily thought about swooning, knew she wouldn't attempt it, hoped to tease him, and instead chose to sigh in blissful joy as he gazed lovingly into her eyes.

Epilogue

"Lottie?" Garrett whispered in her ear as he placed a gentle kiss on her cheek.

Rolling over in bed to see her husband, she thought it strange he was already dressed for the day. "Did I sleep late?"

"No, the sun is not yet up."

She pulled her blanket up further and closed her eyes. "Then why are we awake? Are you going somewhere?"

The bed moved as he sat next to her. "I am taking you out for a surprise. But you will need to hurry if we are to make it."

Charlotte yawned and rubbed her eyes. This was exciting, she didn't mind her sleep being disturbed for a bit of intrigue. "What sort of surprise, my love?"

"If I tell you, it will ruin my plans. Wake up so I can take you on a very early morning adventure." His voice sounded amused. In her opinion it was far too early in the morning for amusement. "Your lady's maid is waiting to help you dress."

Groaning she let him pull her from the bed. "Pray I enjoy this surprise, husband, otherwise you will regret waking me before dawn."

Dressing quickly, she followed her husband out of the house. They'd been at Skye Manor for over a month and had spent most of it indoors, since it was covered in snow. The manor sat on a rock overlooking an inlet on the eastern shore. When her father first proposed giving the property as part of the marriage settlement, Charlotte was hurt. She thought her father would prefer to send her as far from Wentworth Hall as possible. As far from London as well, because it was more than a week of traveling to arrive at the Manor. But after spending the time with her new husband, she decided it was the perfect home for them.

Cholmondeley Hall would always be the ancestral home of Garrett's family, and they would live there for the majority of the year, when not in London, but she hoped to spend time at Skye Manor in the future.

Garrett led her across the snow-covered gardens, through the paths laden with rocks and ice to stand with her and overlook the ocean. He cleared a spot on a very cold rock, placed a blanket over it and pulled her down to sit next to him. She shivered as he wrapped her in his arms and pulled the blanket tight around them. Then he pointed up to the sky.

"Can you imagine sleeping while lights dance across the night sky?"

It was beautiful. The green, purple, and yellow lights moved among the stars in a rhythm. Charlotte had never experienced anything so majestic. Laying her head on his shoulder, she whispered loud enough for him to hear, but softly so it didn't ruin the ambiance. "I do not ever want to leave this little heaven we have here."

"Ashby sent a letter he wants us in town for the opening of spring season."

Charlotte pulled her head off his shoulder. "He has Arundel to command. You are not his heir."

"My love," Garrett said with a smile, "your indignation on my behalf is heartwarming and astounding. I need never worry about Ashby controlling me when I have you by my side."

Charlotte playfully punched him on the shoulder, "You may laugh today, but I know my father. If we rush back to London as he commands, he will always find a way to bring you for his purposes. You and I will be living at Wentworth Hall the rest of his days attending to his desires."

Garrett nodded his head in understanding. "I will trust your judgement, my dear, as I admittedly know I am in unknown territory with Duke Ashby. I was only raised to be a lowly marquess."

Charlotte gaped at his words, then realizing he was teasing her, she slugged him in the shoulder.

"Ouch!"

"Do not tease me, my lord."

"I realize I have gone from, 'my love' to 'husband' to 'my lord' in a matter of an hour. Please tell me how to take you back to the loving wife I woke with a gentle kiss this morning."

"Promise me we will not leave Skye Manor until we are both ready, then you will earn the title of 'my love' again."

Garrett laughed and pulled her closer. "I make a solemn vow not to rush to Ashby's demands, ever, and we will stay here until we are both ready to leave."

Charlotte gave a searching look, to make certain he wasn't just humoring her. "You promise?"

"With all my heart!"

She lay her head back against his chest and curled into his arms. They watched the lights in silence, the cold morning air not bothering either one as they spoke of their fortune at having each other, their future, and the possibility of raising children in such a magical place.

"Promise me," Charlotte said resting in his warm embrace, "we will always be this happy."

"I promise." Garrett's words warmed her heart.

She knew they'd have to put all their effort into making the marriage work, but it would be well worth the time. It would be a marriage of love and devotion to each other, and they would be happy.

Angela Johnson has a love for the written word and the adventures one can take while reading. She loves to travel, read, write, and spend time with her family. She adores her nieces and nephews and loves spending time with them.

A native of Utah, Angela loves the mountains. She believes snow is meant for romantic moments as it lightly falls and melts before it hits the road. Angela believes through reading a person can experience an eternity of adventures.

Find out more about Angela Johnson and join her newsletter at www.angelajohnsonauthor.org.

Points of Discussion

1. What are some of the themes you noticed in *Saved by Scandal?*

2. Which character(s) can you relate to?

3. A key theme in this book is hope. How can you use the example of Garrett, Charlotte, and Ruby to remain hopeful when all seems to be going opposite of what you desire?

4. Charlotte believes in soul mates. What are your thoughts on that subject?

5. What was your favorite moment in the book? Why?

6. The characters in *Saved by Scandal* learn their choices and actions have consequences. How could they have made better choices and caused themselves less heartache?